White Thighs

WHITE THIGHS

Alexander Trocchi

BLAST BOOKS
New York

White Thighs by Alexander Trocchi first published in 1955.
This edition © 1994 Estate of Alexander Trocchi

Blast Books gratefully acknowledges
the generous help of Donald Blaise
and Beth Escott.

Published by Blast Books, Inc.
P. O. Box 51
· Cooper Station
New York, NY 10276-0051

Cover design by Beth Escott
Interior design by Laura Lindgren

Manufactured in the United States of America
First Edition 1994

10 9 8 7 6 5 4 3 2 1

White Thighs

Chapter 1

M y name is Saul. There is nothing in my history nor in my family's history which would justify the name, a significantly biblical one, and in all these years I have been able to discover no shred of reason for the appellation. So be it. I am not one to look for reasons. I prefer the lightning thrust of intuition. The name is like any other and it appears on my birth certificate.

From the beginning I was a kind of stranger. What is that? Ha! Baudelaire came near to expressing it:—

"Your friends?"

"You use a word that I have never to this day been able to understand."

"Your country?"

"I know not on what latitude it lies."

. . . *"Well, then, what do you love, extraordinary stranger?"*

"I love the clouds . . . passing clouds . . . over yonder. . . the wondrous clouds!"

There is no fact which does not appear to me to be at bottom absurd. My father was drowned at sea. He lived "at sea" also. My mother died shortly afterwards of some obscure internal complaint. She always complained and she was always obscure about the origin of her complaints. Thus, from my early years, I was an orphan.

Shortly after what the local parson—a man of certainties—called "this double catastrophe," I was sent to America, where, until the death of my uncle, I grew up. Something which my aunts called "grave" happened there. Aunt Jenny in particular was of the opinion that I was "marked" for life. I have no personal opinion on the matter. And she, surprisingly, didn't know . . .

❦

Aunt Jenny was a goldfish.

Aunt Lutetia was a bluebell.

Uncle Harris was over sixty with long hollows in his cheeks and long grey pants and he was always nervous about something.

Aunt Lutetia was a bluebell because her hat was like a bell drawn tightly over the flat yellow shoots of her hair. It was a blue hat she bought at a Christmas sale and she never went without it.

The reason for Aunt Jenny's being a goldfish was less obvious. She smelled of old lavender and always gave the impression of being powdered with gold dust. Then there was her way of saying "oh" as a fish does, her thin lips circular and her blue eyes round and vacuous. And her skirt sloped inwards as far down as her ankles so that she might have been a mermaid if she had been younger and more beautiful. As it was, she was a goldfish.

Uncle Harris was an American, as he was never tired of telling people, especially other Americans. When Uncle

Harris stepped into the buggy he swung one long grey ranging leg after the other in a manner which suggested he was aware of his movements. When Uncle Harris died it was because he swallowed a dose of rat poison thinking it was something else.

The trees in the park were elms, very green, and so tall and stately that Uncle Harris swore they were planted before white man set foot in America.

They were part of an unspeakable past, prehistoric, because savages, Uncle Harris said, were not in history, and, for the tribes of Indians who roamed there, all time was present. That was the difference between a tribe and a society, he said. A society was change-conscious. Its lifeblood was an ideal. It learned its lessons from the past and looked to the future. A tribe was not like that. It was static, and such progress as there was was unconscious. When Elmer Lewis said one evening that modern Americans were perhaps not quite as conscious as they thought, Uncle Harris was very angry. The elms represented an old order. Uncle Harris owned them.

Elmer Lewis was one of our neighbors. He lived in a fine old house of the colonial style which had belonged to his family since the beginning of the nineteenth century. He was not married and on his death the house and the lands would pass into the hands of a cousin in Boston. He was a cripple, and perhaps that was the reason he never married and that he spent most of his time in the library or experimenting with his orchids. He came to visit Uncle Harris twice a week to play chess. During the game Uncle Harris would allow no one to disturb them. He took his chess almost as seriously as his politics.

3

I remember the lake and the evergreens, the clear white winters when snow covered everything. And I remember the tiny clearing in the copse where I saw Anna of the white thighs give herself to the man.

Anna was not an American, not yet anyway, and in Uncle Harris' eyes she never would be. She was a Jew. The Jews were not a nation and so there was no question of their changing nationality. They were a race whose racial atavism prevented them from being integrated into any nation—a tribe. People knew this, Uncle Harris said knowledgeably, and that was why they called a female Jew a "Jewess." An American woman was an American. Any fool could see the difference.

Aunt Jenny and Aunt Lutetia believed with Uncle Harris, although, believing in one God who was a Democrat, they would never have admitted it. The excess of their kindness to Anna was a kind of penance they did for being so comfortably gentile.

Elmer Lewis avoided the subject whenever possible, but it was difficult for it was one of Uncle Harris' favorite topics of conversation. Together with what was decadent, what was Jewish was un-American.

Anna came to America from Odessa in the Ukraine. Her first memories were of black cargo ships and foreign seamen, Greeks, Turks, Armenians. Her father had been shot by soldiers of the Czar. She herself had escaped from a batch of women seized for a military brothel. That was her mother's fate. She did not know where the rest of her family were.

She learned English quickly and by the time she came to us she was almost fluent. I was ten years old at the time and my aunts, seeing how well-behaved I became in her presence, decided to use her almost as a governess instead of a maid. She was given a room next to mine in the old wing of the house and if Uncle Harris disapproved of her presence there and of her influence on me, he kept silent about it. As I was to discover, he had his reasons: she was for him too, perhaps, Anna of the white thighs . . .

The goldfish and the bluebell told all the neighbors that Anna's father had been murdered by "the red devils." My poor aunts were confused about many things.

Anna became very fond of me. When I was not at school, I was with her all the time. She played with me as though she had been a child of my own age—I think she was twenty-two or twenty-three then. We pretended we were Apache Indians and we tracked each other all over the grounds. Our favorite hiding place was the little clearing in the middle of the copse. It was utterly secluded and no one from the house ever came there. It belonged to us. If, for one reason or another, one of us was detained in the house, we met there, two Apaches who had escaped from the reservation.

After the first summer, my whole world revolved about Anna. Anna was young and full of life. She laughed at me and kissed me. It was she who wakened me in the morning and put me to bed at night. During the day I held her hand and allowed her to decide what we should do. If she stopped to talk to one of the stablemen I became madly jealous and pulled at her skirt to drag her away until she laughed and said to whomever it was who was trying to make a date with her, "It's no use, sir! You see, I'm beholden already!"

Anna was not anything. She was not a goldfish and she was not a bluebell nor anything else. I could not find anything to call her which would have fixed in my mind the smoothness of her olive skin, the way she blinked her dark, heavily lashed eyes, the tilt of her breasts and her wonderfully soft movements.

I would have died for her.

She was all the more wonderful for me as a child because, at the beginning at least, I could only guess at the limber body which moved supplely, with a suggestion of cloying rhythm, under her dress of washed cotton.

One day towards the end of that first summer we were alone together in the middle of the copse. I was lying on my back looking at the wide blue sky and Anna was sitting cross-legged beside me.

"Anna," I said, "do you like America?"

"Yes," she said, "I like it very much."

"Better than Russia?"

"Russia I love too," she said. "There are things in Russia that I miss."

"And do you like Americans?"

"I like some Americans," she said. "I like you."

I laughed. "Oh, I'm not really an American! And I'm an orphan like you. But do you like Americans better than Russians?"

Anna laughed too, then.

"It is *you* I like," she said. "It is not Russians or Americans. It is you, you silly boy!"

After that we did not speak for some minutes. I was going to school in a few days' time, east, away from her.

The thought of leaving her made me more frightened than I had ever been before.

"Anna, what will you do while I'm away?"

"You will soon be back."

"And you'll wait for me?"

"Yes," she said, gazing through the bushes, "I wait for you."

"But I mean longer, Anna!"

"What is it you mean?"

"I mean until I grow up so that we can be married."

She looked at me and laughed merrily, and then, sensing that I was in earnest, she raised her wonderful eyebrows and drew me close to her.

"Yes, my little darling, that is what *I* mean!" And she kissed me on the mouth with her soft red dangerous lips.

But almost immediately she stood up.

"Come, my lad," she said—that was what Uncle Harris always called me—"we carve our initials on a tree. That makes it true, doesn't it?"

We chose the tallest elm halfway up the front drive-way. Anna took the penknife that used to be my father's and with her thin strong hand she cut our initials deeply and indelibly into the bark.

That pledge was the beginning . . .

By the time I was twelve years old my infatuation with Anna had reached an intense pitch. I nursed it like a seed, something nurtured in the dark, out of other people's ken.

Its growth was uncontrollable, but only in the sense that, after a time, I lost the power voluntarily to make it abate, and not in the sense that I was unable to control it in its overt manifestations.

I learned that craft early.

I learned to indulge myself and derive my satisfactions without either awakening the suspicions of my aunts or causing Anna to turn against me. She was sometimes impatient with me, perhaps bored, for she was already mature and longing as any young woman of her age for the experiences of a male, and that, unfortunately, I was unable to provide for her. But there were other things I could do.

I was quick to note that she liked to be stroked, although the type of caress that I was able to bestow on her was not dangerous enough to be wholly satisfying to her. Obviously, in spite of the fact that I had a strange curiosity to do so, I could not feel her under her skirts without raising all sorts of resistance in her. I tried once, pretending to pinch her knee while we were lying in the copse. Her knee mocked me with its smooth perfection. I would like to have kissed it. When I pinched it, it moved upwards in a kind of reflex movement, revealing a few inches of her dusky white thighs, but, as the formless sensation of hunger rose within me, her hand grasped mine and she said: "Don't touch me there! It's not nice!"

I had to be careful.

No. My knowledge that she liked to be caressed was derived from the fact that she always allowed me to brush her hair. She would allow me to do this for hours on end.

I said a moment ago that I had to be careful. I don't

mean that I had to be careful to avoid all sex; just that any sexual gesture on my part had to be cloaked; it had to be made under a smoke screen of innocence, or better, under the interpenetrating smoke screens of innocence and utility.

Take the brushing of her hair. No possible guilt there. And also, her hair had to be brushed. I believe I could have put my mouth to her sex if I could have brought to such an act enough innocence, run through by even a vague utility. For my darling Anna was hot and it was my passionate desire to be the priest of her deliverance.

And so I began by brushing her hair.

A barber does not only brush hair. It occurred to me very soon that none of the normal acts of the barber was forbidden to me. I could massage her scalp, or gently behind her ears, my small fingers drooping at her neck, clinging like a little bee to sticky pollen. I could even stroke her cheek and I was able to put a world of sensuality into that simple action. And when the barber had outrun his limit, I became a masseur.

For that game to begin, I had only to take her gently by the scruff of the neck as I pretended to make the motion of raising her hair. Her head would immediately droop forward and she would usually exclaim: "Oh, my neck muscles are so tired!"

"Yes, Madam," I would say, aping the barber. "If you will just step through into the other room . . ."

And she would do so, not literally, but making a motion with her shoulders to signify her consent.

With warm oil I would massage her neck and the gently moulded muscles of her shoulders—this especially when, on warm sunny days, we lay together in the clearing in the copse. She allowed me to push her blouse up as far as her neck. And then I would massage her smooth back, the heels of my thumbs pressing at her spine. It was only when the tips of my fingers slid under the elastic of her knickers and pressed on the heavy buttock muscles that she made a little movement of resistance to signify that I was moving beyond the limits of innocence. And yet she would have liked me to go on. I knew that because of her heavy breathing, because of the relaxed thrust of her thighs under the cotton skirt.

Subtle as a spider, I would reverse motions, alternately teasing and retreating, teasing and retreating, until her breath came urgently and her pores seemed to emanate a growing smell of woman. At such times, I would lean as close as possible to her, with my head a few inches above her back, and breathe in the smell of her fresh sweat. She was a mine of beautiful sensations. I am not sure she realized how entirely such experience of her dominated my horizon.

It was only in the copse that she would ever allow me to touch her legs, out there, screened from the rest of the world, under a warm sun which made everything languorous. But even then, I could only touch at the calves, and perhaps two inches above the knees if she pretended to doze. From there on the territory was sacred and I crossed the border at my peril. I think that when I did so her annoyance stemmed not so much from her moral indignation as from the anger arising from a strongly felt necessity to order me to stop, and even to punish me by prohibiting me to continue with any form of caress.

But I soon learned a trick of getting around this too. It was difficult to teach her, but after all I was simply offering to be the instrument of her own desire.

One day I said to her: "Just to prove I want to be obedient, Anna, I want you to punish me if I'm bad."

"I will. You don't have to tell me that!"

She had missed the point.

"I mean just as Uncle Harris does."

"How?"

"I want you to slap me."

"I don't want to hurt you."

"No," I said hesitantly, "but it doesn't really hurt on the bottom, not for long anyway."

I saw the faint signal of comprehension in her eyes. That was surely very moral. Punishment, discipline: it was praiseworthy on my part to demand it of her!

The first time, she did it with my trousers on. That was not really satisfactory. We were both aware of the problem. We had to find some good reason for taking my trousers down, one which would not only agree with the positive aspect of morality, but one which, by overshadowing the sexual implications of slapping another person's bare bottom, would be compatible with its prudent aspect. This was not easy. I pointed out to her many times that it would hurt more if she took my trousers down and that therefore it would be a more effective punishment. She agreed but hesitated all the same. It was not until I pointed out to her that sometimes she hurt her hands on my trouser buttons that she finally capitulated.

I remember that first time very well, when, my trousers pushed down about my ankles, I leaned over her thighs, feeling their warmth through the faded cotton dress at my crotch, exhibiting my pink bottom to the wide gaze of the sky. She slapped hard, hard enough to convince herself it was a punishment she was meting out and not a pleasure she derived. But strangely, the more it was obviously a punishment, the more pleasure my beautiful Anna appeared to reap from the ceremony. Toward the end she would not stop until she had brought real tears to my eyes. I always took a long time adjusting myself comfortably across her thighs, and when she had struck two or three blows I would ease my legs apart so that the tender insides of my thighs would feel the sharp shock of her fingers. And so, if after having caressed her for some time I felt her tiring—in the end it is fatiguing to be continually excited without deriving complete satisfaction—I would immediately cross a forbidden border. The more flagrant the offense, the more fierce would be the subsequent punishment. Thus I had to gauge what I wanted to bear. On the first occasion upon which my fingers brushed her short hairs, she made a great sexual effort and lost her temper. That was magnificent!

But even while I suffered the extremest anguish, as her hand rose and fell viciously on my tender buttocks, even as I eased open my thighs to the extent of baring my small testicles to possible damage, my mind was working overtime on the problem of how to capitalize on the great sorrow she would experience at having hurt me so badly. At last I screamed, the pleasure of the scream drowning for an instant the pleasure I took in the beautiful solution I had found to the problem of making this a Pyrrhic victory for her moral fervor. And then, all at once, she was contrite. My face streaming tears, I threw my head against her breasts, forcing with my face and mouth until I had broken a button on her blouse and thrust the already loose brassiere down far enough for me to take her nipple in my mouth.

After her first shock, she gave way. Could she punish me again? A moment later, her arms moved round to cradle my head where it lay. "My baby! My baby!" I heard her whisper.

For a while things progressed by themselves without more effort on my part. The second time I touched her pubic hairs, this time brushing the wet lips themselves with my fingers, the second time she was able to lose her temper, the second time I threw myself shuddering to her breast, I found to my delight that she was wearing no brassiere. And so I realized that Anna had become my accomplice. The rubbery tit was sweet and good in my mouth. My hands closed around the breast and crushed it to squeeze every last drop of imaginary juice. This time she allowed herself to fall backwards on the ground, holding my head firmly in place between her hands. The sun was falling and the copse was partly in shadow and there was the warm buzz of insects and I remember a clump of dandelions not far away. After a while one of her hands slipped away from my head and out of my sight. Her breath was coming in spasms. I felt her torso become involved in minute undulations and I knew she was feeling herself. But when I tried to move down with one of my hands, she stiffened, pushed me away from her, got up, and walked away without saying a word. This time I had really gone too far. She was willing to do anything, but it was my job to find the smoke screens, to find the ethical drugs with which she could put her conscience to sleep. I had not done so. The wall of righteousness was not to be penetrated without stratagem.

It was some time before I was able to take the final, nunlike vows . . .

Chapter 2

*I*t had been Uncle Harris' ambition to be an historian but for the first thirty-five years of his adult life he had been a lawyer. That was the family business. My grandfather had been a lawyer and my father, before he was drowned, was also a lawyer, although he practiced in England and not in the United States. Uncle Harris had been on the point of retiring for many years, but it was only after my arrival that he finally did so. At that point in his life, he moved from law into history like a tornado.

He spent each morning now in his library, making notes for the first section of his great work.

His progress was slow, but it was the first section, he explained on many occasions to his sisters, which would give the stamp of originality to the whole work. The first section (to be entitled "The Concept of History") was to be a kind of telescope with subtly arranged lenses which for the first time would make it possible for contemporary man to look at the past and see it in its true perspective. That was why he would feel justified in spending even ten years in its preparation. For the rest of the work, he would merely have to train his powerful telescope on the works of his predecessors, an undertaking which would not take more than three years, less likely, to rid civilization once and for all of a turgid mass of ancestral delusions. When he spoke, he was very impressive, and my aunts and their friends were duly impressed.

"It's his trained mind," the goldfish said apocalyptically.

The only person in our circle of acquaintances who did not appear the least impressed by my uncle's historical acumen was his crippled friend, Elmer Lewis. This annoyed Uncle Harris because he was well aware that Lewis was no fool. It was all very well to impress the bluebell and the goldfish and the inconsequential ladies and gentlemen who came to take tea with them, but after all Uncle Harris was intelligent enough to realize that such praise meant very little. Lewis was different, for he had traveled widely in his youth before his accident and, since then, for over twenty years, he had devoted most of his time to reading. And Lewis made no secret that he considered Uncle Harris' theory of history a piece of evangelical nonsense. Periodically, therefore, Uncle Harris could not resist attempting to convert his friend to his own opinion.

One summer evening more than two years after Anna came to us, Uncle Harris and Elmer Lewis joined the rest of us in the sitting room. They had been playing chess, and from the condescending manner in which my uncle ushered his friend into the room I surmised that Uncle Harris had won. The goldfish and the bluebell greeted Lewis cordially. Whenever he came they went out of their way to mother him.

Anna, who had been sitting by the window with me, went out of the room after a moment to make some cocoa for us. The rest of the servants had already retired.

"She's such a sweet girl," the bluebell said.

Uncle Harris nodded. "Yes," he said. "It's a pity she's a Jew."

The goldfish and the bluebell looked at the carpet. I said nothing because at twelve years of age I was not expected to say anything, but I thought that if that was so then I wanted to be a Jew also so that nothing could ever come between us.

As for Lewis, he was looking angrily at my uncle.

"Why?" he said. "What possible difference can it make?"

"Read history," Uncle Harris said.

"I have been reading history for forty years," Lewis said dryly.

Uncle Harris smiled and a faint flush of excitement came to the cheeks of the bluebell and the goldfish. Lewis was only a boy, a dear sweet boy, to be sure, but so innocent and naive beside the man who was still the titular head of the family law business!

"My dear Elmer," Uncle Harris said, "in all honesty I think you must bow to my judgment in matters of history. Don't take offense if I suggest that there is only one scientific way of looking at history."

"Abracadabra," Lewis said.

Uncle Harris flushed.

"I have told you before," he said, controlling himself with some difficulty, "that the greatest impediment to the true understanding of history is ancestor-worship. It normally takes the form of awe at old things, a sentimental reverence for trinkets . . ."

"What exactly are you trying to prove, Harris?"

"I don't intend to say any more at the moment than that the Jews are the epitome of what I'm talking about," Uncle Harris said. "They are a decadent race whose whole orientation is unconscious and uncreative."

Lewis shook his head impatiently.

"Decadent, uncreative? What on earth do your words mean? Look at Anna, my God! Is she decadent or uncreative? You are the ancestor-worshiper, Harris. You've got direct contrary evidence in front of your eyes but you won't see it! You're not an historian, Harris. You're an evangelist!"

If the goldfish and the bluebell had been birds they would have twittered.

"Stuff and nonsense!" Uncle Harris exploded. "Take my elms! Take my 'awe-inspiring' elms! Where's my ancestor-worship toward them, eh? No, Elmer. My attitude is scientific. To me, they are timber!"

"Not yet, I hope," Lewis said with a smile.

"As soon as I give the word!" Uncle Harris said.

"Now, now, Harris," the goldfish said. "The poor trees!"

"Yes, Jenny, timber! Timber that will go to create ships, bridges, the structures of civilization. That is progress, a conscious purpose, a movement toward an ideal! I must say I'm surprised and disappointed, Elmer, that you should accuse me of the very attitude I have struggled against all my life!"

"I'm sure Elmer doesn't mean *that*, Harris!" the goldfish said from her best of all possible worlds.

"The most dangerous attitudes are the unconscious ones," Lewis said quietly.

And there the conversation ended because Anna entered the room carrying a big yellow jug of hot cocoa and the company remembered that she was the person around whom the argument revolved.

We drank our cocoa in silence. I don't know whether Anna sensed she had interrupted something, but as soon as I had finished my cocoa she suggested it was time I went to bed.

"Yes, my lad," Uncle Harris said. "Run along with Anna now. It will be a fine day tomorrow."

I shook hands with Elmer Lewis. I did not need to remember to do it from politeness. It was as though he had fought for me. Then I kissed my aunts and followed Anna from the room.

Before Anna turned the light out, I said: "Anna, could I become a Jew?"

She flushed and looked at me questioningly.

"I suppose you could if you wanted to," she said slowly after a moment's hesitation. "Why?"

"Oh, I don't know," I said. "Can I brush your hair, Anna?"

"Not tonight," she said, and when I was silent, she said: "Go to sleep like a good boy. Good night."

"Good night . . ."

The door closed behind her. I was left alone with my thoughts. I closed my eyes and tried to imagine what it would be like if Anna one day did not resist, if, as my fingers caressed the creamy inner surface of one thigh, slightly above the knee, she relaxed instead of stiffening, allowing her thighs to fall open like a book with smooth pages—what then? There came a softness at the tips of my fingers, a wet breaking softness under a mat of fragile hair. What was it she had deep there at her pit, between her legs, like a furry animal? Did it have a life of its own? Was it a strange beast lying in wait with its heaped softness simply bait for the unwary? I would have given anything to know. I fell asleep, a curtain of softness descending over my senses. My last image was of Anna, her head tilted back, her breasts erect, and, like a vast portal at which I longed to prostrate myself, the soft yet muscled forward thrust of her dusky white thighs . . .

※

Dawn broke early. Uncle Harris was down before me with the rods and the nets.

"Take your breakfast quickly," he said. "There's no time like early morning."

When I had finished eating, the horses were saddled and ready. We rode out along the front driveway as the sun rose over the elms. Uncle Harris did not speak until we had left the park.

"There'll be a dollar for every fish you catch," he said. "If you can land 'em as your father did you'll be independent!" He smiled at me. "But no minnows," he added.

I caught nothing though we remained there for three hours. My mind was not on it.

"Might as well get back early," he said.

We rode back in silence.

It was mid-morning when we arrived. The sun was very strong and my aunts were sitting under a large umbrella on the verandah. I went in search of Anna immediately. Uncle Harris himself seemed preoccupied and did not detain me. She was not at the house.

The bluebell said that she'd seen her go out an hour ago.

I ran all the way to the copse, and then, wanting to surprise her, I crawled silently through the bushes toward the clearing.

A strange sound made me hesitate. It sounded as though Anna had screamed, not in fear or pain, but catching her breath, almost quietly. I crawled forward on my stomach to the rim of the clearing.

And then I saw them together, Anna and the man whom I recognized as the half-caste who worked for Elmer Lewis, a man called Inez, and he was doing something strange and terrible to her and she was not resisting, for her smooth, olive-colored legs were stark naked from ankle to thigh, the knees crooked in the air nervously at either side of him and her bare buttocks twitching on a bed of dead leaves. It was as though under the naked front of the man she were dying a strange death to which she gave herself up completely.

I watched in silence, digging my nails into a broken branch which lay in front of me.

Their breath came hurriedly, in pants and grunts, the man boring down into her with his strong yellow-white shaft and her belly quivering like a jelly between his thrusts. I watched and listened bitterly to the muffled dunt of her heels on the leaves, and the shifting twitch of her cleanly curved lower torso as it swayed ecstatically beneath him.

I knew that Anna was being unfaithful to me. This was what I should have been able to do to her. It was toward this I had been unconsciously moving in my daring caresses. And here, insolently, for the man seemed almost detached as he spoiled my beautiful Anna, was this other male, his hairy front hovering like a falcon about to strike, and Anna, ecstatic, like a dying heron beneath him. It came as a revelation.

This was the thing which I knew existed but had not been able to imagine, the practical maturity toward which my own longing was directed, the thing to which grownups referred only by innuendo. Anna was doing it! I watched the man, his ragged trousers thrust down about his ankles, embedded in her. At that moment I swore that I would kill Inez . . .

But I was unable to tear myself away. I watched, my emotions a mixture of fascination and horror.

Every so often, the hot wet mesh of their pubic parts separated a matter of inches and I had the impression of two hairy maws breaking wetly, the hard cruel tongue of one thrust to the hilt in the soft gullet of the other, and extracted, dripping with the other's dying. Anna's smooth legs were delirious, and each time he drew away from her her soft buttocks rose from the bed of leaves against which they had been clamped during his downward pressure and seemed to follow, stuck over by a brown leaf or two, his upward movement, as though reluctant to allow him to escape. Her brassiere and blouse lay crushed at her throat and her beautiful breasts, the nipples pointing skywards, were free one moment and trembling and crushed under his hairy chest the next.

How I hated him!

And then, no doubt feeling her climax draw near, her hands ran electrically down his back toward the purposive tight bunch of his buttocks, encouraging him to complete his violation of her. I was sick with the knowledge of her willing surrender.

Slowly, I turned away from the pale gleam of their wrestling flesh and crept back toward the footpath. How could Anna do that thing which everyone was ashamed to speak of? Was it because she was a Jew? I don't know why I didn't cry or why, when I came to the house, I walked round about it and up the front driveway toward the elms. I looked up out of my own confusion at the sound of rending wood.

One of the elms was tottering. It creaked, lurched and fell in a slow swishing of leaves, raising dust, directly across the driveway. And then I heard the voices of Uncle Harris and two of the stablemen. I ran forward toward the tree and as I came close Uncle Harris and the two men appeared from behind the foliage and climbed across the felled trunk. The two men were carrying axes and a two-handed saw.

It was *our* tree, the highest of them, into which Anna had cut our initials two years before.

My uncle laughed at my bewilderment. He put his arm around my shoulders and steered me back toward the house.

"How are the mighty fallen!" he said with a laugh. "You see, my lad," he continued when I did not answer, "that was the highest elm for miles around. No one but didn't tell me that. Harris, they said, that tree must be as old as Moses! Well, so it might at that. But what did that prove? To me it proved only that those who said it were a pack of sentimental nincompoops! Because you see, my lad, the old must give place to the new just as the fit must survive. History proves that. That is progress. All in all, that is America, a country of which you'll learn to be proud! I want you to remember. The old is destroyed to create the new. Treat with contempt those jackasses who want you to grovel before what's old an' remember what's old's likely to be decadent an' the decadent's no farther from death than a fly's spit!"

"But the tree, Uncle Harris! It was a beautiful tree!"

"It was an old tree, boy. People opinioned it beautiful. That's as may be. I know now that it's a useful tree." He gripped my shoulder. "Don't let them fool you, lad!"

I did not answer and we walked on in silence

Suddenly he said: "But where's your pretty Anna? I thought you were going to look for her?"

Impulsively, I twisted away from under his arm.

"Look for her yourself!" I cried. "She's in the copse with a man!"

As I ran from him toward the house, the tears were streaming down my face.

In the evening I became oppressed by a sense of guilt. Anna's faithlessness, coupled in my mind with what I considered her great daring, was a very grand thing as compared with my mean betrayal of her secret . . . I felt an overpowering need to confess to her, but when, at last, bedtime came and I was alone with her, I was afraid.

She kissed me good night as usual and I listened to her footsteps as they died away along the corridor.

I could not sleep. I felt that my betrayal of her was only a beginning and that my inability to confess to her so that she would know her secret was discovered and guard against it was like diving in water and not knowing except for the knowledge of the descent itself and the sight of your own hands pallid in water and over-reaching, like broken rudders.

Uncle Harris had not appeared since I ran away from him. He was absent at lunch and at dinner. My aunts said that he had decided suddenly to go into town. They did not know why. From Anna's face I learned nothing. She was as calm and lovely as ever, and yet a few hours before I had seen her naked and writhing in her sweat below the man. Occasionally during those two meals she turned suddenly and saw that I was looking at her. I flushed and turned away.

An hour passed very slowly and I began to know that I would not sleep until I had told Anna what I had done. Perhaps she would forgive me. I would cry and plead with her until she did. All I had to do was to wait until she came upstairs again to go to bed and then I would go to her room.

At eleven o'clock it began to rain heavily.

Some time afterwards, I heard her footsteps pass along the corridor and then the noise of her door opening and closing behind her.

I lay still and waited. The rain beating heavily on the

windowpanes filled me with a vague dread of the dark corridor.

When finally I was about to reach forward with my hand and open the door I became aware that someone was on the other side with only the thickness of the door between us. I could hear his breathing. I should have screamed if whoever it was had not moved away at that moment. The footsteps went along the corridor and once again Anna's door opened and closed.

Who was it? Anna's lover? Inez? A flush of utter hatred passed through me.

Without thinking, I went over to the wardrobe and put on my dressing gown. Then I left my own room quietly and crossed the corridor to the little bathroom beside Anna's room. I moved as quietly as an animal. Inside, I snibbed the door and, without putting on the light, dropped on my knees in front of the keyhole of the communicating door between the bathroom and the room where Anna was.

The sight shocked me. Anna, her flimsy nightdress ripped, exposing her full lovely breasts, was cowering away from Uncle Harris who was standing, still wearing his riding breeches, his feet apart, at about two yards distance from her. He threw a bundle toward her which fell to the floor at her feet, and then he stood watching her, his hands, hanging down in front of him, flexing a riding crop. On Anna's face was an expression of horror.

He said something and she looked down at the bundle.

He was speaking to her quietly and she seemed to be protesting. The word "harlot" came to me. He listened to her, a small smile playing on his lips, and his right hand moved round to his side with the riding crop and he flicked it from time to time against his leather riding boot.

As I could scarcely hear what they were saying, it was like a mime show, the man cool and relentless, the woman desperate. The riding crop moved outwards and pointed at the bundle. Anna seemed to catch her breath and she shook her head frantically. Uncle Harris spoke. The riding crop pointed again and moved up and down in a small arc.

And then, lowering her terrified eyes and staring at the bundle, Anna divested herself of her nightdress and stood bare naked in front of him. She was trembling.

It was the first time I had seen her naked.

Her slim olive shoulders, smooth as satin, were slightly hunched, as though she expected to be attacked, and in that posture her wonderful young tawny breasts with nipples darker, more brick-red, than a rose, were partly obscured from my line of vision. I gazed fascinated at the superbly rounded turn of her sleek belly muscles, of the buttocks tight but full, at the thighs, the dull white inner surfaces of her soft thighs and the strong black-haired mound which I had seen open like red spitting jaws during the morning. So beautiful was she with her black hair falling to her shoulders and her long, slightly yellowish legs apart and run through by the nervosity of a timid animal, that for the moment I forgot all about Uncle Harris. I was utterly weak and doting at the sight of her.

It was only when he moved again, pointing again toward the bundle with the riding crop, that the reality of the situation reimpressed itself upon me.

She was stooping now, undoing the bundle. I fixed my eyes on the pale white thighs below the buttocks, catching a glimpse between her legs of the soft-haired cleft.

The first item that came to her hand was a black suspender belt. She looked at Uncle Harris hesitantly.

He nodded grimly.

Slowly she slung it about her golden belly and hooked it at the soft left side of her waist. Four black elastic straps, each bearing a silver buckle, flapped at her thighs.

Uncle Harris said something, I think to tell her to be quick.

Sheer black silk stockings next. She sat on the edge of the bed to put them on.

Uncle Harris leaned over the bundle and extracted a pair of very high-heeled, patent black leather shoes with complicated ankle straps. He threw them in front of her and she put them on.

He must have ordered her to stand up.

The high heels had the effect of giving a forward thrust to the mound and thighs, like a hungry, seductive gesture, and the two tightened straps at the front framed the sex, black as seal-skin with a thin, coral-red slit.

The next thing he threw to her was a mask, a simple mask of black velvet, as jet black as her pubic hairs.

He flicked the cloth which had contained these things aside with his riding crop.

He spoke again.

Hesitantly, she went to her dressing table, the supple movement of her gleaming flesh accentuated by the black accouterments. She returned with a lipstick.

He pointed with his riding crop at her breasts.

Slowly, with obvious reluctance, I watched her slender hand, like a butterfly, hover over the warm mould of her breasts, and then, slowly, with a care that surprised me, I watched her redden her nipples to a bright carmine. They stood out like a shock against the muddy whiteness of her flesh.

He pointed to a chair.

She stood up on it, displaying her entire wonderful body. And as I felt the dull throb of excitement within myself, I began to understand my uncle's insistence on these elaborate preparations. For Anna had been transformed into a naked sexual object, a woman, a gleaming torso subtly exhibited to the eyes of her despoiler.

But it was not over yet.

Taking the lipstick himself, he walked across to her, and, opening her sex with the thumb and forefinger of his left hand, he applied the carmine to the wet crescents of her labia. Shock red through shock black—he stood back to examine his handiwork.

He moved over to the fireplace, thrust his hand up the chimney, and examined the soot on his palm and fingers. Returning to her then, he touched it lightly on the insides of her thighs close to the sex. The application of the soot heightened the grottolike impression that the smooth thighs lent to the mound, shadowing, accentuating, the carmine-red clitoris which, a few moments before, before the application of the greasy lipstick, had been the color of a sea-urchin's flesh.

It was over. She was naked, or nearly naked, a torso ready for the sacrifice.

His first act was to move close to her, grip her firmly

by her swelling buttocks, and thrust his face, the mouth open and lascivious, at her groin.

She tottered on the chair. But his mouth was glued firmly amongst her pubic hairs and his red cheeks were contained by the white thighs.

Anna had closed her eyes and thrust her hands up to cover her face. She needn't have, for it was already masked with the velvet mask.

He sucked at her for some minutes and when his face came away the bottom part was smudged over by lipstick. He removed this with a white handkerchief.

Then he must have ordered her to pose for him, for, without warning, she went into innumerable alluring poses. I marveled at her beauty.

Another gesture with the riding crop.

Slowly, she climbed off the chair, turned, and stooping slightly, gripped the bottom board of the bed, so that her creamy round buttocks, stark white above the black stockings and scored by the black straps of the garter belt, were presented to him. He said something. She nodded miserably, her long black hair cascading down between her beautiful white arms to the level of her soft pulsing belly. I would have liked to put my own head there, deep in its softness.

More quickly than I would have imagined possible, Uncle Harris stripped himself naked. His member was half hard and his sinuous white right arm swung in a half circle through the air, testing the resiliency of the riding crop.

My eyes returned to Anna. Her buttocks were quivering with fright and her superb carmine-tipped breasts rose and fell with her breathing.

"Ready?"

It was the first distinct word which came to me through the door.

Without looking around, Anna nodded miserably.

After that he didn't hesitate. The crop swung through the air and struck the soft flesh of her beautiful buttocks viciously. She shuddered, her whole warm torso involved in the radiating pain of the blow. And again, this time pausing after the stroke to examine the thin red weal which the crop had made on her shuddering flesh. And then he set to work seriously. Four, five, six, seven, eight, nine, ten. He hesitated. Anna had slipped down to her knees, all huddled up, obviously in great pain.

Brutally, he grabbed her by the hair of her head and threw her backwards over the bed. As it happened, her slender legs pointed toward me, and, as they had fallen apart, I was confronted by the warm, lipstick-soiled clot of hairs at her crotch. Only momentarily, however, for my uncle after one cruel stroke of the crop right at the crux of her thighs could contain himself no longer. With a guttural croak of lust he threw himself huge and rampant on top of her, forcing her thighs wide apart with the bony blades of his own, at the same time bringing down his slack, twisted mouth on one bright red teat which disappeared in his gullet. I watched her struggle helplessly, her legs flapping under him like broken fins, and then, all of a sudden, he bellowed like a bull and spurted his old man's passion deep in her womb. He was on his feet in a trice, and a few minutes later, while Anna, who had turned over, her white buttocks bleeding onto the black harness, was still weeping on the bed, was fully dressed and addressing words to her again. I suppose she was listening, but she made no move to turn around and face him.

He spoke for at least five minutes, eyeing her balefully from where he stood, fully dressed, flicking the riding crop once again against his boot, and then he turned on his heel and left the room. I heard his footsteps in the corridor again. I waited awhile at the keyhole, watching Anna cry. How slack and white her whole torso looked with its provocative black trappings. Even now the high-heeled shoes, strapped to her slim ankles, were on her. One of the stockings was laddered, but otherwise the whole undignified harness was in place. That scene, relived a hundred times in memory, has been an object lesson for me.

Silently I went out into the corridor.

Terror in footsteps receding, in the opaque glimmer of the corridor and window, in the wet sound of the night, in my own heartbeats as I pressed my ear against the panel of Anna's door, and then the small sound of her sobbing through the wood—quietly, unable to suppress altogether the strange elation I felt, I opened the door. She lay there still where he had left her, her soft body bereft of all purpose, quivering with shame and outrage.

"Anna!"

I ran over to the bed and pulled her face round to me. It came as a shock to look directly at the black velvet mask with its diagonal almond-shaped slits, the eyes like dark wet pools glimmering below.

"Oh, Anna, I'm sorry!"

It was a long time before she spoke and then her voice

was subdued and toneless. We were lying in the soft warm darkness of her bed, my naked body pressed close to hers, except where I felt the stockings and the garter belt she hadn't bothered to remove, and my head was on her shoulder and my hands clutched at the soft odorous flesh of her armpits.

As she had emerged from the copse in the morning, she had noticed Uncle Harris standing under a tree not far away. He was smoking and he was watching her. She passed quite close to him but he made no move to restrain her. As she walked away from him toward the house she felt his eyes following her and she was frightened.

Then he did not appear all day and she was sure something was going to happen.

She had just got into bed and turned off the light when Uncle Harris entered the room. He did not knock. Without warning he switched on the light. He carried a riding crop and the bundle and he was breathing heavily. She knew at once what it was he wanted to do. She told him to get out but he laughed and said she need not pretend to be virtuous to him. *He* knew. He might have known before. She was a slut, a common little whore whom he had fed and protected. And before the night was out he was going to show her what a whore she was. He dragged her from the bed, tearing the flimsy nightdress away from her trembling breasts.

"But if you had screamed, Anna!"

"He said he would have me deported."

"Send you away?"

"To Russia. I'm not an American citizen," she said bitterly.

"But you could tell!"

"He is a judge. Who would believe me?"

I said nothing for a moment. With one small hand I was massaging her warm belly. A strange, exciting odor arose from it to my nostrils. She made no move to stop me.

"But you're all right now, Anna," I said at last. "Don't cry any more! I thought he was going to kill you!"

She seemed even to like my soft caress.

There was a strange harshness in Anna's laugh.

"Do you think he won't come again? He'll come every night now! He said I would have to get used to it. Every night now I'll have to lie awake and wait for him to come until I can't stand it any longer and then when I'm desperate enough I'll kill myself!"

"No, Anna!"

Even in the darkness I felt she was looking at me almost hatefully. My hand froze just above the matted hairs of her lower belly.

"No, Anna!" she repeated derisively. "What then? Shall I kill *him?*"

"Would you?" I said nervously.

All this talk of killing frightened me and fascinated me at the same time. It was part of a new strangeness which surrounded Anna. I remembered what I had seen in the copse. Was Anna different from other women? Were all women like that?

"Why not?" she answered coldly. "Why shouldn't I kill him? Do you think I like him doing that to me? *I hate him!*"

"Let *me* kill him, Anna!"

The words seemed to have spoken themselves. But remembering my thoughts on Inez during the day, I was only half terrified at what I had said.

She laughed and ruffled my hair. It was a tired laugh. My hands twitched again near her hot, hairy chevron.

"My little Apache!" she said. "If only you were a man and not a little boy!"

"I'm not so little! I could do it!"

Part of myself remained detached, listening, like a witness.

"Silly boy! Why should you kill your own uncle? He's kind to you . . ."

"Because I hate him too and it was my fault!"

"Your fault! How?"

I was trembling as I told her what I had done.

For long minutes she said nothing and I was conscious again of the rain on the window. I closed my eyes to shut everything out of myself and I became gradually more intensely aware of the soft shock of naked flesh against my own. On the tender undersurface of my right wrist, where the veins pulse, I was aware of the hot bowl of her young, sweat-lathered, outraged belly—my fingers were now amongst her pubic hairs—as it rose and fell with her breathing. Her strange female odor entering at my tense nostrils seemed to enter my very veins like a paralyzing drug and I was overcome—a dull, witless sensation at my groin—by a terrible lassitude. I felt a terrible need to be absorbed by her.

"You!" she whispered softly.

"It was the tree, Anna," I said tonelessly. "He was cutting down our tree . . ."

She did not seem to hear me. My slack lips opened near her armpit and, breathing inwards deeply, I sought to annihilate myself with her odor. Seconds passed, the rain shattering against the window in gusts.

"And you *could* do it . . ."

Her hand pressed mine against the wettened hairs of her sex.

"Nothing would happen to *you* . . ."

I didn't answer. The sudden utter knowledge of her warm protective nakedness had driven all resistance from me. She was looking straight up into the darkness.

Her voice came to me.

"You want to be mine, don't you, Saul?"

I rubbed my face against the warm plasticity of her breasts.

"And you will do it, won't you?"

When I didn't answer she went on in firmer tones:—

"You *must* do it for me because then I'll be able to forgive you for what you did and everything will be all right again, everything. You must . . ."

I had closed my eyes again and I said "yes" over and over again until it became easy to say it and I was an outlaw in her world with her.

"You love me, don't you, Saul?"

In the silence, in spite of my terrible promise, I felt warm and sure, as though in a physical way through contact with her warm, wounded body I were drawing on her courage and her purpose. She was turning toward me, her soft thighs coming against my knees. I saw her face smile in the dark. I felt the pressure of her hand on mine.

"Touch me harder . . ." she whispered.

She guided my fingers between the slime-hung rims of her bristling sex.

"Feel," she said. "Explore it gently . . ."

The sticky mucous stuff felt like wet, warm cellophane between my fingers. I felt her hand at my genitals, tickling, caressing. She kissed me wetly on the ear.

"Ah! you're too young for that . . ."

I hardly heard her.

"Show me you love me . . ." she whispered, and, very gently and persuasively, she took my head between her hands and forced me down until her hot, urgent odor mingled with her wet short hairs at my lips and nostrils. She raised one warm, infinitely heavy thigh, and forcing my mouth against her dripping slit, lowered it again, cutting off sight and sound. I was now lying upside down, far beneath the bedclothes, my own little member between her firm young breasts and my head gripped between the sleek white jaws of her thighs. Vaguely I heard her say that I belonged to her, and then: "Suck . . . suck . . . suck . . ." The repeated word measured the rhythm of her desire. All was lost. The nightmare was over, my will first paralyzed and then, as it were, taken over. I loved her frantically. I existed only for her. My mouth devoured her greedily. At that moment I became her creature . . .

If Uncle Harris had had a sense of smell he would have known that there was more than black currant wine in the glass. And if he had not made a practice of gulping things he would not have swallowed enough rat poison to die.

I think he had a moment of clarity just as he

screamed and clutched his throat and staggered back into the armchair. And even then he was not dead and the horrified blue eyes were staring at me out of the helpless body which took such a long time to die. And we looked at each other, both of us horrified at what I had done.

My aunts heard the scream and came downstairs and into the library for the first time I remember without knocking.

"Harris!"

The bluebell was there first slapping the paralyzed hand and calling his name at him, Harris! Harris! Harris! and the goldfish ran to the telephone and called Dr. Meadows to come at once because Harris had had a stroke and then they were both there kneeling and slapping like two old peasant women washing laundry.

The dead man still breathed through a fallen mouth which had lost the power of speech and after a moment the eyes left off staring at me and stared fixedly upwards. Uncle Harris was looking at his eyebrows.

Uncle Harris was dead when Dr. Meadows arrived and the doctor, after examining the body, turned with a serious expression on his face toward my aunts. They were seated stiffly at the edge of the settee and never for a moment had they taken their eyes off their dead brother.

"Jenny," Dr. Meadows said, "I wonder if you and Lutetia would mind making a cup of tea or something? There's nothing more to be done and I would like a word in private with the boy."

They got up obediently, like puppets, and left the room.

"Well, Saul?" he said when they had closed the door behind them.

I felt myself blushing and looked away from him. I didn't speak.

He lit his pipe with great deliberation.

"I wonder if you can tell me anything about it, Saul?"

"How should I know?" I cried. "He was old! How should I know anything about it!"

He did not speak for many minutes. He seemed to be arguing with himself. He walked across to the window, looked out, and teased his long nose between thumb and forefinger. When finally he turned round again, he said quietly: "You will hide this from the others Saul, but you cannot hide it from me. I know. Do you understand? Now will you tell me why?

I was silent.

"I must know why, Saul."

I gritted my teeth and remained silent. We were staring at each other, much like Uncle Harris and I had stared at each other while he slowly died.

"Will you speak?"

I shook my head.

"All right," he said resignedly at last. "Now, run along to bed and as you go tell your aunts that *I* will make arrangements for an undertaker."

As I opened the door to go out, some childish impulse made me say: "How did he die, Dr. Meadows?"

"Very painfully, I should think," he answered dryly.

During the days before the funeral Anna avoided me. I felt like a leper. When I reproached her, she said that it wasn't safe for us to speak. She made me swear over and over again that I would never mention her name in connection with my uncle's death. She explained that they would do nothing to me but that if she were implicated they would take her away and put her in prison. I promised. That night she took me to bed with her and allowed me the same freedom with her body. With each new experience of her I became more entirely her creature.

And then, on the day of the funeral, Anna disappeared.

Driving back from the old town in the company of my aunts, the bluebell told me that Anna was gone. She had eloped, she said, with a servant of Mr. Lewis'.

Inez!

"So soon after his death!" the goldfish said. "It shows you, Lutetia, how you can be mistaken in people!"

"Harris always said . . ." the bluebell began.

"Where is dear Elmer?" the goldfish said diplomatically, with a glance toward me.

I had seen Elmer Lewis at the graveside, a lonely figure on his crutches. He was the last to leave.

In the house, I ran upstairs to Anna's room. It was utterly empty. I stood there until I saw myself in a mirror.

In my own room I found an envelope with my name written on the outside in her big childish script. I opened it eagerly, but there was nothing inside it but a lock of her soft black hair. I burst into tears.

Two days later the hair sizzled in the match flame and I had to draw my fingers away quickly to avoid burning them, and then I was down on my hands and knees searching frantically to save a few strands but there was nothing left except the pain at my fingers and a few flakes of ash on the lavatory floor . . .

Chapter 3

I suppose it was Dr. Meadows who advised my aunts to send me back to England. For themselves, I am sure they would have preferred to keep me in America. They spoke vaguely of my health. They seemed to be moving and making decisions in a dream.

I was nearly thirteen when I sailed back across the Atlantic. I never saw my aunts again for they were dead when I returned to America ten years later.

Of the period between, I shall speak only briefly. I went from school to university and by the time I was twenty-two I was a Bachelor of Arts. For ten years I followed the conventional course, studying desultorily, passing examinations, playing a little sport, reading, and occasionally going out with a girl. But without exception I despised the girls I met; they were pretty, docile, and unserious. Nothing touched them to the quick and they had no more effect upon me than the idiot boys with whom I was forced, at school and college, to associate.

Had I not after all killed a man?

I felt myself to be . . . different.

There could be nothing for me in what others called "love"—where was the risk? I despised civilized affections, the soul-destroying "matey" quality, the sugar-sweet tendernesses of the liaisons between boys and girls of my own age. What I sought after was something much more terrible, something which could be described as a commitment, intense, obscene, even criminal, and undertaken, assented to religiously, as a nun defines herself by her vow. Indeed, up till that time, except for my experience with Anna, I was as chaste as any nun. On my twenty-second birthday, I had still not known a woman. The only woman I had ever met who measured up to my peculiar standards was the one who was ever present in my belly like a dark pencil of lust from the time I committed murder for her.

Anna haunted me, always evasively—the white thighs, a ripple of olive-tinted flesh and a fleck of black hair disintegrating in my dreams. I would lie awake at night, the flesh of my belly crushed cruelly between my fingers, aching in every nerve to feel her flesh close, possessing me, and to feel her will move in me again. Would she still be the same? Or would she have become soft, spavined, fat, cowlike, in the ten years which had passed since she used me for her fatal lust? I didn't know.

The fact that she would be ten years older, a woman past thirty, excited me tremendously. If she had not gone to seed, if she had preserved that vital quality of contempt, her dark purity, the green fury of her passion, then how much more easily, and with how much more subtle calculation, would she be able as a mature woman at the height of her powers to take possession of me and make me her own consecrated instrument!

For that is what she had made of me, and the wax,

once set, was firm and unchangeable: I experienced no desire to possess nor to mould in my own likeness but an urgent necessity to be annihilated, used again even to the point of murder, and to draw identity of every act done of *another's* necessity. The memory of Anna electrified me. She alone of all the women I had met was fit to receive such homage. Had she not made me commit murder for her? I nurtured the memory like an orchid, an extravagant, dangerous orchid, with as much loving care as a poet gives to his creation. I worshiped her. I imagined myself prostrate before her. I buried my head between her soft thighs, knowing their strength. I asked her to judge me, to control me, to administer my punishment. I loved her, called to her in my dreams that I would kill my uncle all over again. She *had* to exist. She could not be dead, or worse, grown weak and insipid as the women I met at college. That would be a betrayal. Men have destroyed gods for less.

But my doubts remained. Ten years is a long time, and had I met another woman to whom I could have brought the same religious dedication I should without doubt have committed myself afresh. I even attempted to do so.

On my twenty-second birthday I traveled to London for a week's holiday. The idea had been growing in my mind for some time. Surely in such a huge city as London I would be able to find such a woman? Somewhere, I had to find her, for by the act of poisoning my uncle I had delivered myself over to an obsession.

I was walking along Piccadilly when it occurred to me that I might find my woman among the hustlers who plied their trade there. I had few illusions about a chance meeting with an unprofessional girl. None I had met so far had been remotely like the woman I was looking for. But a prostitute—a prostitute surely had to have some metal in her. I halted at a corner and glanced at the people who were passing by. It was already dark and as the weather was cold the people were muffled up to the ears. Nevertheless, it was easy just because of the cold to tell which women were going somewhere and which were not. I counted three prostitutes and considered them one by one. The first was a slim dark-haired girl, rather pretty but also rather pathetic, I felt, with her rabbit-fur collar and little pageboy cap. The second was a tired-looking peroxide blonde, about thirty-five, who was constantly stamping her feet on the pavement to keep herself warm. It occurred to me that she would be better off in a brothel. She didn't attract me. The third woman was different. She was a heavily-built woman with a big bust, good legs, and coppery-red hair. She looked healthy and as strong as a horse. She, too, was over thirty, but probably a year or two younger than the blonde. I decided to approach her.

She smiled as I came up.

"Short time, luv?"

I nodded.

"Three quid," she said, looking me up and down.

I nodded again.

She beamed, and when she did so I nearly walked away. I didn't want this kind of attitude. But I decided to go through with it. When I had her alone in a room I would try to get her to understand. Nevertheless, I didn't hold out much hope.

I followed her through a number of backstreets and into an entrance beside a newspaper shop. It was ill-lit. Instead of mounting the stairs as I had anticipated, she led me under them into a dark corner.

"Do it here, luv," she said.

"Have you not got a room?"

"Cost you another quid," she said.

"Is it far?"

"Just around the corner."

"Let's go then," I said.

She nodded and went out ahead of me. Again I had an impulse to turn back. By this time I was certain that I had chosen the wrong woman—perhaps the young girl, after all . . .

We turned the corner and went into an entrance and up a narrow wooden staircase. On the third floor she knocked at a door with a large brass nameplate on it. We stood for a long time before it was opened to us, first on a chain and then wide to allow us to pass in. It was an old woman with grey hair and a wart below her left eye who let us in. She pointed at once to one of the rooms on the far side of the hall. My prostitute nodded and, indicating with a motion of her head that I should follow her, went in.

It was a smallish room with a four-poster brass bed. She pointed to it and I sat down. Then she carefully locked the door. When she turned again she was beaming. She came across to me.

"Present first," she said.

I gave her four pounds. She tucked them away neatly in an inner pocket of her handbag. Then she removed her coat, revealing her large-busted figure in a green woolen dress.

She began to strip.

I watched, fascinated.

Her thighs were fat and the color of damp chalk, wounded where the split sex, almost unhaired, lay open like a mass of pale calf's liver. Her belly hung down over it in a rounded fold, abrasive as rough sandpaper where the hairs had been shaved. Crabs probably. She had not removed her brassiere.

I was sitting on the edge of the bed and she was standing about two yards away. I had to summon up all my courage to spread out my arms, wider than her hip span, implying without speech that she should move forward from where she stood. She did so slowly, her big blue-pink knees betraying her hesitation.

And then she halted, the ambiguous mass of her sex about six inches from my face. At that distance, every terrible flaw in her skin was visible, the pitted areas, the places where the fragile networks of veins lay close under the skin.

"Satisfied?"

For a moment the question made no impact upon me. It hovered beyond my comprehension, like an irrelevant minor motif in a bad painting.

And then, suddenly, I understood.

She had misinterpreted my desire. She thought I was examining her for purely utilitarian reasons. She had no notion of sacrifice, no acquaintance whatsoever with the sacred. I was at that moment confronted by a big stupid cow submitting dutifully to a veterinary examination! I seized her angrily by the hips to check her retreat and thrust my face squarely between her thighs. She emitted a gasp of astonishment and, grasping me by the hair, forced my head away.

For a few seconds, she looking down, I looking up, we regarded one another balefully. I hesitated no longer. Raising my feet and planting the soles of my shoes firmly in her soft, sagging belly, I kicked out with all my strength.

She cried out as she hurtled backwards across the room, big, ungainly, shock starting in her eyes. Her head struck heavily against the edge of the dressing table and, with the sound of air escaping from a soft tire, subsided unconscious on the floor.

I crossed over and looked down at her. Then, with my ear pressed against the door, I satisfied myself that the old woman had not been alerted. There was no sound.

I turned back toward the unconscious woman. Some unusual quality in the crooked abandonment of the limbs made me excited. I felt as though I were on the threshold of a discovery. Somewhere outside a clock struck seven. I approached her without articulate purpose.

Now that she was no longer conscious, no longer free to intrude her vulgarity, she was beautiful. The heaps of pink and white flesh had a warm life of their own.

With my penknife I cut through the tag which joined the two bags of her brassiere. I laid them aside and gazed down at the breasts. They were heavy, pulp-white, and filigreed with tiny red veins. The nipples were as big as olives, and crinkled as olives sometimes are, tough, chewable. I took her left nipple in my mouth and sucked it. She didn't stir.

A moment later I was on my feet again. The torso had the strange humility of the sacrificial lamb. It was a new experience for me, to have at my mercy another's body in this way. I was the priest, invested temporarily with the powers of deity, and she the brute material out of which in some act or other of piety I was at liberty to . . . what precisely?

Yes, everything depended upon my skill, or rather upon my knowledge, my intuition. But there *was* no sudden illumination. And it was the absence of such an illumination that made me hesitate. I was in a state of awe, of lust, of frantic expectancy. I could feel myself growing hard. But what act would bring about the urgent, the mystical resolution? What does one do with one hundred and eighty pounds of unconscious female flesh? What act would express the fluency of knowledge?

The naked whore, unconscious, spread-eagled clumsily on the dirty red carpet, her breasts sagging now that the cheap pink brassiere had been cut away—these were the facts, the police-court details, to which one could react in any number of ways. I could have called an ambulance or I could have thrown a jug of cold water over her—more police-court details, and not at all the kind of thing to assuage the strange unrest which had been a prominent feature of my life ever since the death of my uncle.

Priest? I sat down disconsolately on the bed again. A priest without knowledge of the sacraments. What was the use? I stared almost hatefully at the sprawling woman. But I could not bring myself to go just then.

Instead, I sat down beside her and laid the palm of my hand flat on her belly. I allowed it to ride with the movement of her breathing, up, down, up, down, and as I clenched my hand, smooth hot dough, pulsing, living. I laid my ear at her belly and listened to the rumbles within. She smelled quite clean. I opened my trousers and took out my penis. Then, supporting myself with my hands, I lowered the hot mass onto her soft, puttylike crotch. It felt good. Leaning my whole weight now on that part of me, I joggled about on top of her until I felt the spasm approaching. Then, carefully, and breathing heavily, half-afraid she would recover consciousness, I opened the lips of her sex and laid myself just inside. I grasped her big buttocks, threw my weight forward, and in three tremendous lunges brought my vital juices smoldering into her belly.

I felt better after that. It had been an interesting experience.

I withdrew, washed myself in a flowered china bowl, and arranged my clothes.

Now there was nothing for it but to go. Why waste more time? Anyway, she was beginning to stir and I had small mind to have a hysterical woman on my hands. She might even send for a policeman, or worse, for her pimp.

I opened the door quietly and gauged the distance to the door across the quiet hall. There was no one in sight. I hesitated no longer. A moment later I had let myself out the front door and was climbing once again down the flight of stairs.

As I walked again through Piccadilly it occurred to me that it would have been possible to kill her . . .

That was the last time I tried to come to terms with myself or with my strange passion while I was in England.

The half-abortive experience with the prostitute weighed on my mind during the following months. In May of that year I completed my studies and wrote to Elmer Lewis saying that I had now decided to return to America and that I intended to live on the old property.

After the death of my aunts, my uncle's estate had passed entirely to me, or rather, it was to be held in trust for me until I attained the age of thirty. Elmer Lewis was one of the trustees.

He replied at once saying that he looked forward with great eagerness to meeting me again and that he hoped I would always consider him as a counselor and a friend.

I traveled on the *Queen Mary*. The voyage in Cabin Class was entirely uneventful. I spent most of the time in my cabin occupied with two distinct but allied questions. In the first place, I was anxious to know whether Dr. Meadows was dead and whether he had died keeping my secret. Secondly, I was curious to know whether Elmer Lewis suspected (or knew) the truth, and, if so, what his attitude toward me would be.

Lewis, as I well remembered, was a highly intelligent individual and it was not at all unlikely that he had surmised the truth about Uncle Harris' death. Would he hold the boy's crime against the man. From the tone of his letter, it didn't look like it. He might know, but if he did he still seemed willing to overlook what had happened. It was not that I gave a damn what Lewis thought. I didn't require his approval for any fantastic theory of history. But as he was one of the trustees it was in his power to keep me extremely short of cash during the next eight years. I always had expensive tastes and I had only six thousand dollars a year at my disposal. More than that depended entirely upon the approval of the trustees. And so it would be to my advantage to make a friend of Lewis even though it would be out of the question for me to make him my confidant.

My confidant!

Dear old Elmer Lewis! What would he think if I told him of my intention to search out Anna wherever she was and to make some kind of unholy alliance with her? What if she was married? She might have married Inez. Yes, I remembered Inez . . .

What if she had children?

I was ready for all such eventualities. I would allow nothing, no one to stand in my way. Such a strange and immutable purpose was not likely to recommend itself to a dyed-in-the-wool liberal like Elmer Lewis. It would more likely have appealed to my dead uncle.

The thought made me smile.

It was my first intimation of the fact that in some ways my late uncle and myself were alike . . .

I had not expected to be met at New York.

The skyline of the city rose on the horizon out of the early-morning mist like matchboxes open and shut. As we left the Statue of Liberty astern I descended to my cabin to make ready to disembark. A steward approached me with a cable on a tray. I tipped him and entered the cabin to read it. It was from Lewis. It said shortly that he was meeting the boat.

All the better. Somehow I felt relieved to know that I should meet him again for the first time on neutral territory. If he had not already planned to do so, I would persuade him to spend one night in New York before setting out for Vermont where my late uncle's estate was located. I would pump him as expertly as I could. I wished at once to know three things:—

Was Meadows dead?

Did Lewis know the truth about my uncle's death?

And, where was Anna?

I was very excited. I couldn't remember being so excited in a long time.

The familiar figure on crutches was waiting for me as I passed through customs. He looked older. His hair was white. But it was the same round, benign face with small well-modeled features, and watery grey eyes which looked kindly out from behind small gold-rimmed spectacles. The whole impression, in fact, was one of smallness. He was a smallish man, with small hands and feet, and as, leaning forward on his crutches, he stretched out both hands to contain one of mine in his, the impression one had was of limitless love and good will.

"Glad to see you again, my boy! It's been a long time! Ten years, dear me! Makes quite a difference. You've grown up to be quite a man!"

I laughed as naturally as I could and returned his

warm handshake. But I was uncomfortable all the same. This little scholar had seen right through my uncle. I should have to be very careful if I didn't wish him to see right through me.

"Well now," he went on in his fussy way, "let's see!"

I waited for him to go on.

"Yes," he said. "Now I have my car outside. Traveled here by car, you know. Easier with these pins of mine to be driven. Can't stand trains! John—that's my chauffeur—is outside with the car just now. Let's see . . ."

I relaxed. It would be better to allow him to make any plans that were to be made. I would do my utmost to give him the impression that I was a well-mannered young man with the appropriate respect for my elders. And so I walked slowly along beside him without interrupting, an expression of polite interest on my face. A porter followed with my bags.

"I'm staying at a small hotel in Manhattan," he proceeded. "Thought it might be a good idea to spend the day together in New York . . . get to know one another, ha! ha! . . . and then get a good early start in the morning. How does that strike you? Not too impatient to get back to Vermont, eh, my boy?"

"Just as you wish, Mr. Lewis. I'm glad to be back. It's pleasant enough just to be back. I'm not in any particular hurry to do anything, to tell you the truth!"

"Ha! ha!" Lewis twinkled. "Glad to hear it! You're like me then! Never was in a particular hurry to do anything! Give me leisure, my books, and a few friends, and I wouldn't change places with a Sultan!"

It was an unfortunate alternative. I disagreed with

him entirely, but in reply I simply laughed and nodded.

The shining Rolls-Bentley was waiting at the curb. The negro chauffeur saluted and opened the door for us.

"Climb in, my boy!" Lewis said. "You first. Easier that way with these confounded crutches!"

I did so and then the chauffeur helped his employer to get in beside me. The bags were loaded in the boot and then the car started up and moved into the stream of traffic.

"Back to the hotel first, John," Lewis said to the chauffeur.

"Yes sir."

Lewis turned his attention to me again.

For a moment he said nothing, simply studying me from behind his spectacles. I felt he was on the verge of saying something very important. He was.

"I want you to know, Saul—you don't mind my calling you Saul?"

I shook my head.

"Good," he said. "I want you to know that I know how your uncle died."

His eyes flickered behind his spectacles. It struck me that they were an asset to him. The lenses were so shaped that in certain lights it was difficult for the person he addressed to see his eyes. He, on the contrary, was able to see the other's eyes quite clearly. I felt myself reddening under his gaze.

"I tell you this at once," he went on, "because I don't wish our relationship to start off on the wrong foot. I want to put your mind at ease. I didn't want you to be obsessed with the question: Does old Lewis know or

doesn't he? You know now that I know, that I understand, don't condemn, and that your secret is safe with
me. And so that should get rid of any horrible suspicions
between us."

"Dr. Meadows told you?"

"He told me just before he died. He thought it was
better that I should know."

Inwardly I cursed Meadows. Once a murderer, always
a murderer. I could imagine the old fool's reasoning.
Watch that boy! He might do it again! The fact that his
reasoning was valid made the situation worse. Lewis
would reason in the same way. I felt he approved of
Meadows' disclosure. He would watch me carefully.

"You are the only one who knows?"

"Except Anna, of course."

"Anna!"

"Yes," Lewis went on. "I imagined at the time that
she must have had something to do with it. You were very
much under her influence. I took the liberty of ques-
tioning her. She told me everything."

"I see."

"You see, I knew that you wouldn't have done anything like that by yourself. Dear me, no! You were quite
fond of your uncle. He wasn't altogether a bad man. In
fact he was my best friend."

"I'm sorry," I said mechanically, without looking at
him.

He reached out and put his hand on my knee.

"But it's all over and done with, Saul," he said. "I
want you to know that. Unless you feel like discussing the
matter, I shan't refer to it again. You're a man now and

you have all your life ahead of you. You must try to forget. What happened then is no longer important."

How blithely he said it! I wondered bitterly if he believed it.

As the car turned out of Fifth Avenue I asked him where Anna was now, making my voice as casual as possible.

"As a matter of fact she lives not far from your place. With her husband. She married a man called Inez, an old groom of mine. I don't know whether you remember him."

Did I remember him! The man in the copse!

I feigned ignorance.

"It was a long time ago," I said quietly.

"Of course! Dear me, you can't be expected to remember everything!" He hesitated before he went on. "As a matter of fact," he continued, "I told Anna you were coming. I suggested that it might be a good idea if she left the district. She agreed. She said she would talk to her husband. He's a poacher. A drunken lout. I was gravely mistaken in him. No good to God or himself. Poor Anna!"

"I don't think it matters," I said more purposively than I had intended.

His eyes flickered.

"You mean that she goes away?"

"Yes," I said. "After all, it's a bit thick to ask her to get up and leave just because I arrive . . ."

"Perhaps," he said reflectively. "But I really don't believe she cares one way or the other and I intend to make it worth her while. Don't worry about her, my boy! She can take care of herself."

The old meddler! Why couldn't he mind his own stupid business? So she didn't care! Well, we would see about that!

I pretended to have lost interest in the subject. I didn't want to arouse his suspicions.

"Did my aunts ever know?"

"Poor dears, no. Meadows thought it best not to tell them. Meadows took a risk, you know. He could have got himself into hot water. Accessory after the fact, don't you know."

"I suppose so."

"But then he was an old friend of your uncle's, a good old family doctor. He had courage." He hesitated. "Well, anyway, it's over now," he said with a small laugh. "It's best forgotten. And here we are, this is my hotel. I've already reserved a room for you. I'm sure you would like a bath. Nothing like a bath to help you relax, eh?"

The car drew up outside a small but expensive-looking hotel. The doorman moved out from under the blue and white striped awning, saluted, and opened the car door.

Chapter 4

*T*hree days later I was seated alone in my late uncle's library. How strange it was to be there in those familiar surroundings, looking at the long curtains of red velvet, the shelves of leather-bound books, the inlaid chess table with the red and white Chinese chessmen, the heavy desk of oak, the oils of Bingham and Cassat, and the log fire blazing in the hearth. It was not really cold enough for a fire, but I had given instructions for it to be lit all the same. It made the room more cheerful. I was seated in front of the fire in my late uncle's big winged chair, reading a volume of Poe, one of my favorites.

Since my arrival, I had explored the grounds, penetrating even into the copse where Anna and I had so often lain together during those bright summer afternoons, and examined the stump of tree, now blackened by wind and weather, *our* tree, which Uncle Harris had caused to be felled because he was afraid of its antiquity. Indeed, there was nothing of former significance which I had not minutely re-examined.

It was nearly midnight. The servants were all in bed.

Lewis had left two hours before. He had dined with me that night. He had spoken of Anna.

She and her husband, Inez, it seemed, planned to move to Georgia in three weeks' time. Lewis was sorry he had been unable to get them to leave immediately. He was sure that I would have preferred it that way; such a painful link with the past was better broken at once. Unfortunately, however, the house they were going to in Georgia would not be vacated for another three weeks. Well, there it was. Meanwhile, he suggested that it would be better if I didn't see Anna.

At that moment I began positively to dislike Elmer Lewis. If he thought he was going to arrange my life for me in accordance with his own skim-milk precepts, he was mistaken. I intended to visit Anna the very next day. Lewis could think what he liked.

I was glad, however, that the departure had been delayed for three weeks. That would give me ample time to change Anna's mind for her. For I intended to put into operation at once my plan to be with Anna, and it would be much lees trouble to have her in the neighborhood than to be forced to search for her in the state of Georgia.

I thanked Lewis warmly as he left for his kind attention to this affair of clearing Anna out of the neighborhood. I don't think he caught the undercurrent of irony in my voice. When he was gone, I called Mrs. Kelly, the housekeeper, to the study and posed a number of questions to her. I apologized for bringing her down.

I told her that having been away for a long time and that as I intended now to settle down on the estate I wanted to hear what had been going on in the neighborhood during my absence. I asked a few innocent questions to begin with, questions the answers to which didn't interest me in the slightest. Then I asked her about Dr. Meadows, pretending not to know of his death. She told me he was dead.

"Poor Dr. Meadows!" I exclaimed. "He was our family physician, you know. He was very kind to me when I was a boy."

Mrs. Kelly nodded sympathetically. I had created a good impression on her since my arrival.

"And there was a girl, at least a woman," I continued. "She was my governess for some years. Anna was her name, I think. I wonder what ever became of her?"

Mrs. Kelly had pursed her thin lips.

I raised an eyebrow, questioningly.

"She's still in the neighborhood, sir, at the old Cromarty place," said my housekeeper after a pause, "—with that husband of hers. Inez, they call him. An evil man if you want my opinion!"

"Oh? Why do you say that, Mrs. Kelly?"

"Oh, there's been many stories, sir," said Mrs. Kelly in her old-worldly way. "Not that I listen to gossip myself, but there's no good in that man. Ask anyone."

"What does he do for a living?"

"Steals. He's been chased off your grounds more than once, sir, for poaching. I don't think he's done a hard day's work in his life!"

I smiled. "He's often about these grounds, then?"

She nodded, almost triumphantly, I thought.

"And what about Anna?"

Again this middle-aged Irish woman whom Lewis had employed to run the house during my absence pursed her lips.

"A woman who'll put up with a man like Inez . . ." she began.

I waited for her to go on.

She was flushed, as though Anna's behavior came to her as a direct personal insult.

"Well, sir, there's not much I can say. But she's hardly the type of woman I'd invite to my house if you take my meaning."

"Perfectly, Mrs. Kelly," I said blandly, making a mental note that I should have to get rid of this disapproving old bitch at the first opportunity, "but tell me, do they have any children?"

She shook her head.

"Miss Coogan—that's the district nurse—is a good friend of mine. There's been three miscarriages in that house in five years. Not that I'm suggesting anything . . ."

I nodded.

"Well, thank you for bringing me up to date, Mrs. Kelly. You've been most helpful. I've been away for such a long time I'm out of touch with everything."

"Oh, there's a great deal more to tell, sir," Mrs. Kelly said enthusiastically.

"I'm sure there is," I said quickly, "but I don't want to keep you out of your bed any longer. In fact it was very inconsiderate of me to call you at this hour . . ."

"Not at all, sir, not at all!"

I smiled. "And anyway, I have some important letters to write. Must attend to business, eh?"

"Yes, indeed, sir!" Mrs. Kelly chirped.

"Good night then."

"Good night, sir."

When she had gone, I poured myself a glass of brandy and settled comfortably by the fire. So Anna lived in the old Cromarty cottage? Well, that was interesting. It was not more than a hundred yards from the east boundary of the estate. No wonder Inez was tempted to do a bit of poaching from time to time.

In the morning I would ride over and see her.

What would she be like? I could hardly contain myself. At this moment, her beautiful white thighs relaxed, she would be sleeping not more than half a mile away. To think of it! I felt as an old voyager must have felt when his sailing ship after perilous adventures in foreign ports and on the high seas finally sailed up the home sound.

I closed my eyes.

"Anna, my darling, I am coming to you . . ."

At breakfast, to keep my mind off things, I made an inventory of my servants. There were six altogether, not many for an estate of this size, but all were new, that is to say, they had been selected by my counselor and friend, Elmer Lewis.

Mrs. Kelly without question would have to go, and the sooner the better, for even if she were to prove faithful to me rather than to Lewis, I could not bear her moralizing and her thousand and one old adages. And anyway, she had proven herself unfriendly toward Anna, her future mistress, unwittingly doing herself out of her job.

Then there were the two maids, the one who served at table, a breathless little brunette with soft, provocative haunches, Milly Brown, pleasant enough and even interesting, and Mona, a thin redhead with green eyes and a very pale complexion, who acted as chambermaid. Of the two, I was more interested in the latter. She had a strange, elfin quality about her. Well, for the moment, I would keep them both. With Mrs. Kelly out of the way, I would have a better chance to get to know them.

As for the cook, she was a fat blonde Swede, whose name was Kirstin. She looked like a masseuse, was about forty years of age, and from the look she gave me when I first entered the kitchen was just the kind of woman I wanted in my employment. Kirstin was all right, and from what I had gathered in the short time I had been home, I surmised that there was no love lost between her and Mrs. Kelly. All the better. Kirstin could stay.

The other two were men. As there were only two horses now, a grey mare and a black gelding, neither of them of particular value, there was not enough work for a full-time stableman. One of the men, Henry, looked after the horses and acted as gamekeeper. I didn't like the look of him. He had fair hair, freckles, honest blue eyes, and looked as though he would have been shocked by a pair of French knickers. That kind of man, I could hardly retain in my service.

Cliff, on the contrary, appeared to be just the kind of man I wanted. He was dark, with a low forehead and narrowly-spaced eyes, and he seemed to be a deplorably bad gardener, that is to say he knew nothing of his job and would probably not be averse to making up for it in other ways; just the type of mean wretch who could be bribed, and who, if his services were well rewarded, would think twice about opening his mouth to anyone. I liked Cliff. He was very rightly suspicious of a world in which he was forced to earn his living as a gardener, especially as he had probably never seen a garden before his arrival on the estate. He looked more like an ex-jailbird. And so I decided that Cliff could stay.

By the time I had finished shuffling all this over in my mind I had finished breakfast. Now it was time to go to see Anna. The reorganization of the household could wait until the afternoon.

I sent Milly with instructions to Henry to saddle the mare, and ten minutes later I mounted and moved off at a canter down the front drive. I glanced to the left at the black stump of the elm as I passed. Well, there were other elms, and there would be plenty of time to cut our initials over again.

67
𝕊𝕊

𝕊𝕊

I came out through the wood directly opposite the little cottage where old Cromarty and his wife used to live. I reined in the mare and sat still in the saddle, gazing at the trickle of almost colorless smoke which sidled up from the red brick chimney. Anna lived there. I had arrived at last . . .

I urged the mare on at a walk, savoring those last few minutes which led toward the woman to whom I was eternally bound, to whom I had committed and recommitted myself each night before I slept. I would allow nothing now to stand in my way, not Inez, not Lewis, not even Anna herself. I would *make* her accept me.

Suddenly, as if to greet me, I saw Anna step over the threshold with a wooden bucket in her hand. She had walked out a few paces before she saw me. She put down the bucket and stared.

I dismounted, and without waiting to tether the horse, walked quickly toward her.

"Saul!"

"Anna!"

A moment later we were fast in one another's arms.

"Oh, Saul! You shouldn't have come!" she whispered through her tears.

I kissed them away, allowing my whole body to lean against this soft, but powerfully muscled woman, and my hands ran up and down her back, caressing, loving.

"Come inside!" she said suddenly. "Someone might see us!"

I allowed myself to be led by the hand into the cottage.

As soon as the door closed behind us, I took her in my arms again and crushed my mouth against hers. Her full lips opened and the hot wetness of her mouth mingled with my own.

"You've grown up," she whispered as soon as she managed to free her mouth. "Oh, Saul, it's so good to see you!"

"Darling," I said between kisses, "I've come back to you . . . I belong to you! . . . I'll never leave you again!"

"Oh, Saul!"

She freed herself and sat down on a chair.

"It's no good, Saul, it's no good! You know that! They'll never let us be together!"

My jaw tightened. "Who's they?"

"Oh, you *know*, Saul! Inez and Mr. Lewis . . . neither of them would allow it!"

The hair rose at the back of my neck. I held out my hands, palms upwards and fingers spread.

"I'll strangle them with these hands!" I said quietly, and I looked into her eyes.

"Don't talk like that!" she said quickly. "Oh God, you should never have come!"

"Anna," I said quietly, "I killed my uncle for you. You asked me to show you that I loved you. I worship you! You have no right to ask me to live without you . . . As for Inez and Lewis, let me take care of them!"

"Oh no, Saul!"

I laughed suddenly.

"It might not be necessary to kill them, Anna!"

And then she was laughing too, and I sank down beside her chair and laid my head in her lap. I felt her fingers moving in my hair and I felt relaxed, utterly.

"Little Saul!" she said almost to herself. "I never thought you would grow up!"

"I've grown up for you, Anna . . ."

"Yes," she said, her fingers tightening in my hair, and then, simply, she added: "For me."

When she said it, I lifted her cotton dress up over her white thighs and exposed her naked sex with its shell-pink clitoris and gleaming black hairs. The thighs were fuller, the same dusky white, with the same sweet smell of fresh sweat that I remembered. I was kneeling between them, gazing with adoration at the soft milky tub of her lower belly down which now, as she had matured, a fine spine of black hair ran, from her navel to her crotch. I leaned forward and with little nibbling kisses, like a sheep grazing, moved my lips down from her broad, sweating belly to the hot, mucous, hairy mass at her crotch. She twitched in her chair, her soft white buttocks shuddering, slithering forward to bear her pulsing lust deep into my mouth. Only the small of her back now remained in the chair. Her buttocks, thighs, and legs jutted out horizontally and I supported them in my arms. Mad with desire now, she held my head firmly at its doting work, and her heavy thighs closed about my ears, the buttock muscles tightening, of urgency, of necessity.

Gently then I drew her onto the stone floor, my mouth still buried deep in the rising fluids of her crotch, and I felt her buck, and buck, and buck, as she rose on my worshiping tongue to her first whimpering spasm.

The pressure of the thighs relaxed then, and rolling me onto my back, she squatted over my mouth, with little pulsing movements making her passion-soaked hairs dance on my lips. My tongue swayed under her soft, hairy cleft like a charmed snake, and I was hungry for her to descend so that I might again contain the soft, dripping flesh in my mouth.

She stood up, allowing the skirt of her dress to fall down and obscure her thighs.

"Come over to the bed," she said. She was breathing heavily and looking down at me strangely.

I followed her over.

She slipped out of her dress and unhooked her brassiere. Then she lay down, entirely nude, on her back on the bed.

I was now able to examine her body. It had thickened. The muscles had become heavier over the years. The hairs at her soft, almost pudgy armpits she had allowed to grow, thick, black, and coiling like soft strands of wool.

She was looking at me, curious, appraising.

"Lick me all over," she said softly. "Start at my toes."

I laid myself down beside her and bent my head over her left foot, tracing a spiderweb caress on the hard skin of her soles, rising or falling suddenly between the toes, feathering across her instep, to her ankle and to her beautiful swelling white calf. I was out of time then, doting, annihilated and geared to her will, tasting each hair, each pore, its sweetness and its sweat. And soon I was moving up again, past her dimpled knees and within the soft white gate of her thighs. At that moment, she raised her knees, allowing my tongue access to the tender under-thighs, the smooth chubs of flesh where legs and torso joined, and to the lemon-yellow crevice against which the blue-black hair was smoothly set. Round on her warm spreading belly next, all senses at the tip of my tongue as it traced for the second time the fine line of hair between sex and navel. Fine hairs, like dust almost, clung to the slabs of flesh below her rib cage. I moved softly over them, like a careful gardener with a mower.

"My breasts . . ." she whispered huskily.

I approached them from one side, up from the satin-soft hollow of her hip. Her breasts were fuller than I had known them, rounder, but still firm, and the teats, in spite of the fact that she had no children, had been developed to the size of smallish grapes. She breathed outward heavily as I took one of them in my mouth and sucked avidly. I was transported, wrapt entirely in the warm body of this woman to whom I had chosen again to be committed. Her hands clutched at my hair, urging me to put every nerve of a doting power into my homage. When the breast was erect, I moved to the other one, applying my lips abandonedly to the sweet nipple.

"Take off your clothes . . ."

As quickly as I could, I divested myself of them entirely. And then, naked, and with a more urgent erection than ever before I laid myself almost breathless beside her.

She raised one arm, exhibiting the soft mass of hair at her armpit.

"Under my arm . . ."

I teased and parted the hairs with my tongue, seeking the pink-white flesh beneath, grazing my cheek against them as I might have rubbed against a cat.

She turned over and kissed me passionately on the lips, her dark eyes open and gazing curiously into my own. Her smile, when our lips came apart, was suggestive.

"Do you love me, Saul?"

"Do you not know I do?"

"How do you love me?"

"I worship you, Anna!"

She almost purred. Her eyes twinkled with amusement.

"Lick me again, first," she said.

I hesitated for I didn't know what she meant until she moved upward slightly in the bed and swung one heavy white thigh over my shoulder. I felt my face crushed against her sopping wet sex. And then her thighs tightened as though she meant to strangle me.

"Suck me!" she commanded.

Once again my mouth broke into her smooth, slimy vagina and my straining tongue made doting pressures against its walls. Her warm breath was deep. One of my hands lay on her soft white belly.

"I remember the first time you did this, Saul," she whispered between gasps. "I had forgotten that you belonged to me . . ."

And with that, she tightened the pressure of her thighs. This time I could actually feel the boiling issue of her sex as it rose to its second climax in my mouth. I sighed deeply and relaxed among the warm pressure of her flesh.

She pulled me up until my mouth was on hers. Her eyes were still open and a faint amusement lingered in them.

"F . . . me now," she said softly.

How can I describe the relief, the ecstasy I experienced as my painful erection was sucked through hairs, through the soft, soapy lather of her lust, deep into her hot pulsing belly! The infinite tenderness of her! The breaking of her heavy thighs as they opened to support my hips!

"Darling . . ."

"F . . . me . . ." she whispered.

I rode there, balancing on her soft gymbals, gyrating

voluptuously with the thick root of my sex crushing against her delirious clitoris. She seemed to enjoy that pressure most of all, her hands moving like fluttering birds on my back. And then, finally, I felt her stiffen beneath me, the lower part of her torso like a huge maw erect, the buttock muscles tight and prising upward, lifting, her hands seizing my own buttocks and gripping them frantically toward her, and her final scream, which began huskily, almost soundlessly at the back of her throat, and rose up through her mouth, gaining momentum, sound, ecstasy, as it spluttered wildly from her full, red, grimacing lips and as though by sympathetic magic caused me to burst like a volcanic gusher deep into her womb.

"Oooooh . . ."

Like a tigress she was up, scratching, snarling, forcing my shoulders flat on the bed with her knees, and then blackness, the soft, seething, pulpy mass of her descending on my face as though to suffocate me. And then, jerking her hips, her fingers clutching my scalp, she painted my face with the overflowing brush of her sex.

We were dressed.

I was sitting in a chair opposite her.

"I can't, Saul."

"But why can't you? Good God, you don't love him, do you?"

She flushed.

"I don't know," she said. "I don't know what I feel.

It's just that he has a kind of power over me, like an animal, like a beast . . ."

"And me?"

"You know I love you, Saul. I've loved you ever since you were a little boy."

I smiled bitterly.

The sound of her voice now made me feel sick. Did she think I had need of sentiment? I began to see at that moment that Anna was not the woman I had created for myself in my imagination. She was another man's woman, his thing. And I began to see what I would have to do. I knew I was in the clutch of an obsession.

"I'm going now, Anna. But remember, I won't allow you to leave the district."

"There's nothing we can do . . ." she repeated in her resigned voice.

I felt a slight twitch within me, like the turning of a compass needle. The situation as I knew very well was not insoluble. I had already come upon the answer.

On the ride back to the house, I weighed it over in my mind.

Immediately after lunch, which was served to me by Milly in the dining room, I sent for Mrs. Kelly and informed her of my decision to dispense with her services.

She was mortally shocked.

"But why, sir! What have I done? I demand at least to know what you've got against me! In all my working days this has never happened to me before! The very idea!"

"And I'm sorry it has to happen now, Mrs. Kelly, believe me. But a man is entitled to choose his own servants. You were chosen by Mr. Lewis, and his taste is perhaps not mine. It's quite simple and there is really nothing more to be said."

"The very idea!"

"I'd like you to leave at once, Mrs. Kelly. I shall instruct Cliff to drive you into town in the car. Of course I shall give you two months' wages in lieu of notice."

"Well, I must say! You have no right to treat me in this way! I have never been treated in this way in my life before!"

"That will be all, Mrs. Kelly. I have neither the time nor the desire to argue with you. You may go now."

"I'll speak to Mr. Lewis about this! You see if I don't!"

"That is entirely your own affair, Mrs. Kelly. Meanwhile, be good enough to leave the premises."

"Well, of all the nerve!"

"G–E–T O–U–T, Mrs. Kelly!"

That did it. She bustled out, calling to God and man to witness her humiliation.

I rang for Milly.

She came in nervously. I smiled. No doubt she had already heard what had happened and would be worrying about her own position.

"Please send Henry to me, Milly."

"Yes sir!"

Henry came about five minutes later, a pleasant expression on his freckled face.

I informed him shortly that I was dispensing with his services.

He took it more calmly than Mrs. Kelly had.

"When do I leave?"

"Today if possible. I will pay you two months' wages in lieu of notice. I'm sorry, Henry, but my mind is made up."

"That's O.K.," he said. "I hear Mrs. Kelly got the sack too. I can ride into town with her."

"Just as you wish, Henry. If you need a reference, write me for it."

"Thanks," he said. "It won't be necessary."

"Just as you wish. Come to the library for your money before you go."

"O.K."

I spent the rest of the afternoon exploring the grounds.

As I was walking back toward the house along the front drive Cliff came abreast of me in the car. He had just returned from town where he had driven Mrs. Kelly and Henry.

He was excessively polite.

"Will you need the car again tonight, Mr. Folsrom?"

"Not tonight, Cliff."

"Then I'll put it away in the garage."

"Do that . . . Oh, and by the way, Cliff . . ."

"Yes sir?"

"That man Inez, is he on the grounds much?"

"I've seen him four or five times in the last couple of weeks, usually at night."

"Does he take much away with him?"

"A few rabbits mostly, sometimes a bird or two, but this is not the season."

"Of course not. But he's around here all the same?"

"Yes," Cliff said. "I saw him last night."

I nodded.

"Chase him out if you see him," I said unconcernedly. "We don't want him hanging around the estate."

"I sure will, Mr. Folsrom!"

And he drove in front of me up the drive, past the house, toward the garage. The old Buick was still a smart car. Anyway, unless Lewis came across with more money, I wouldn't be able to afford a new one.

Almost as soon as I got into the house, Lewis rang.

Mrs. Kelly had been to see him.

"Did you have any particular reason for getting rid of her, Saul?"

"No. I simply wish to choose my own servants."

"Of course, but she's a good woman, you know, very efficient housekeeper."

"That's not the point, Mr. Lewis. I just felt I wouldn't get on well with her."

"Mmm. I think you've made a mistake. I've known her a long time."

"I'm sorry, Mr. Lewis, but you'll have to let me be the judge of that."

"Yes, of course. I simply wanted to know if anything had happened."

"No. Nothing."

"And Henry, was that for the same reason?"

"I suppose so, yes. I didn't particularly like the look of him, that's all. It's very simple."

"I'm surprised you should prefer Cliff to Henry . . ."

I laughed at his consternation.

"I didn't say that. It's simply that Henry struck me as

an independent type of fellow and I don't consider independence a virtue in a servant."

"I see . . ."

"We've probably different ideas about this kind of thing."

"Er . . . yes," Lewis said thoughtfully. "Your late uncle might have said that. He wouldn't tolerate independence in a servant . . ."

"So you see, I'm running true to tradition!"

He chuckled but I sensed an undercurrent of uneasiness in his laugh.

"I appreciate your point of view, Mr. Lewis," I went on. "You are pretty orthodox liberal. My uncle wasn't and as it turns out neither am I. Tom Paine . . . the Rights of Man, all that—it leaves me quite cold. I prefer Nietzsche for example to Bentham or Mill."

"I see . . ."

"I'm sorry, but that's the way it is, Mr. Lewis."

He hesitated at the other end of the wire and then, almost mechanically, he said:—

"Not at all, Saul. Every man is entitled to his opinion, eh?"

"Except a servant," I said, irony in my voice.

He grunted incoherently.

"Silly to discuss matters like this on the telephone," he said, with an attempt to be good-humored. "We'll talk about it some other time, over dinner. Much more civilized, eh?"

I laughed.

"Any time," I said pleasantly.

"Sorry to have disturbed you," he said.

"Not at all. Good-bye for now."

He said good-bye and then I heard the click as he replaced the receiver at his end.

As I laid down the telephone it occurred to me that if it were to be done it would be well done quickly . . .

Chapter 5

*I*t was on the third night of my watch just before dawn that I saw his thickset figure break through the undergrowth.

As on the previous nights, everything had been dead quiet for a long time, with nothing more than an occasional night noise. It was almost windless and the leaves stirred almost imperceptibly. The woods stretched out on all sides and I had the impression of living in another world, a foreign, unknowable world through which tiny night animals burrowed.

I had almost decided to give up for a third time when I heard the strong crackling of twigs and the small commotion of a frightened rabbit as it scurried away from his approach.

Silently, I cocked both barrels of my shotgun, held my breath almost involuntarily, and leaned back out of sight against the tree.

It seemed an age before he appeared.

I was tense. In spite of the chill atmosphere of the dark woods I could feel the perspiration on my forehead. After the strain of my long vigil, my courage had almost seeped away.

Yes, it was he.

". . . like an animal, like a beast . . ." Anna had said in her rich, wondering voice.

It was my enemy, Inez.

As the thumb of my right hand grazed gently across the cocked hammers, feeling them erect, steel, sharp as flint, it came to me that in a few moments now I would pay off an old score which went back to the day in the copse when his act confirmed my terrible destiny. Was the man even aware of my existence? The man? . . . the animal, the beast . . . and I the hunter waiting for him with death in my hands. My excitement grew.

He was so near that in that quiet place I could see the whites of his eyes. He was wiping his broad face with his hand. In his left hand he carried a single-bore shotgun.

A sudden sense of power rose up in me.

From my place of concealment I gazed long and hard at my dead man.

Half an hour before dawn. An appropriate time for an execution.

The gun was hard and cool in my hands.

I spoke.

"Stay where you are! Don't move!"

He froze. The whites of his eyes seemed to grow larger as he peered madly in front of him in the direction of my voice. And as his gun moved up protectively across his chest I shot him twice, with great accuracy, between the eyes.

As he fell forward his own gun went off and the lead shot burst redly out and upward from the barrel, causing nesting birds to shriek and wheel from the trees. I laughed silently as I felt the whip of pellets tear at my shoulder and I could have cried aloud for joy when my hand, touching it, came away bearing blood.

He had wounded me!

I was still laughing nervously and triumphantly as I leaned over his sprawled body to examine the red and bleeding mass that had been his face.

<hr>

"What on earth is it, Saul?"

"I've killed a poacher, Mr. Lewis. He took a shot at me and wounded me in the shoulder. Can you come at once? I've already sent for the sheriff."

"Good God!"

"Please! Can you come?"

"I'll be over right away!"

I hung up.

"Pour me another brandy, Cliff. A big one."

"Yes, Mr. Folsrom."

<hr>

The sheriff arrived first in an old Chevrolet.

Pretending to be nearly overcome with shock, I told him my story.

I had been unable to sleep. I had taken my gun and strolled about the grounds, thinking I might have a shot at a rabbit. In the woods I had encountered the man. I challenged him. He swung up his gun and took a shot at me. I fired twice . . .

He surveyed me noncommittally and said he would go and take a look at the body. I told Cliff to go with him.

"The name's Inez," the sheriff said when he returned. He lit a small evil-smelling cigar. ". . . although, with what he's got left for a face, it's difficult to tell. Fancy shooting on your part. He was a bad devil. Known him for a long time. Knew he'd come to a sticky end sooner or later."

"God! so that's Inez!" I said, collapsing in a chair.

"Know him, Mr. Folsrom?"

I shook my head.

"No. But I hear he married my old governess. That makes me almost a parricide!"

The sheriff laughed.

"No need for you to worry, Mr. Folsrom," he said. "He got what was coming to him. You must have given him a scare when you challenged him. That'd be what started him shooting. He was trespassing and it's a clear case of self-defense."

He made a gesture toward the drink cabinet.

"Help yourself, sheriff," I said.

He nodded casually and helped himself to a long shot of rye whiskey.

He looked at me, almost smiling. I feigned nervous exhaustion.

"Of course, there'll be an inquest," he said, "but that'll be a matter of routine. He was well-known around these parts. A sinister bastard. Yeah, Inez . . . boy, you sure messed up his face!"

I winced.

"Here," he said, "let's have a look at that shoulder."

Fortunately, I didn't need to simulate pain as he helped me off with my coat. He cut away my shirt and examined the wound.

"Nothing serious," he said slowly, "but you'd better call a doctor. Some of the shot's gone quite deep. Near shave, I'd say. Might have blown your head off as you did his. You were lucky."

The white flesh of my shoulder was punctured and lacerated in many places, red spots and grey where the pellets had embedded themselves under the skin.

"Yeah, you sure were lucky!" the sheriff said. "Inez was a sharpshooter."

I nodded.

"Lucky you were ready. Lucky he didn't see you first!"

"This might not have happened if he had! He would probably have simply slipped away."

"Yeah, I suppose so . . ."

"It's a funny feeling, sheriff."

"What's that?"

"To have killed a man."

He gulped his whiskey and knocked the ash off the end of his cigar.

"A fraction of a second you'd have been the stiff, Mr. Folsrom. No. You did right. You plugged him right between the eyes. I'd have done the same in your place."

"Thanks. It's nice to hear you say that. It makes me feel much better."

He laughed. Then he got up and went over to the telephone.

"I'll ring for an ambulance," he said, "and I'll tell them to send a doctor at the same time."

While he was on the telephone the doorbell rang.

"See who's there, Cliff."

"Yes, Mr. Folsrom."

A moment later Mr. Lewis burst into the room.

"Dear me! What on earth's happened?" he said excitedly, and then, catching sight of my wounded shoulder, he cried: "My dear boy! Are you all right?" He hurried across to me on his crutches and gazed in bewilderment at my shoulder.

"I've killed Inez," I said slowly.

"Inez! Good God! Whatever happened?"

The sheriff intervened.

"You'll be Mr. Lewis?" he said.

Lewis nodded, gazing from me to the sheriff.

Concisely, the sheriff explained what had happened. From his lips, the story sounded absolutely watertight. I could have embraced him.

"My poor boy!" Lewis said when he had finished. "What a terrible thing to happen so soon after your arrival!"

I thanked my stars for the wound in my shoulder. Obviously Lewis had swallowed the story without question.

"But think of poor Anna!" I said miserably.

Lewis seated himself on a chair.

"Poor girl! poor girl!" he repeated.

"That his missus?" the sheriff said without emotion.

"Yes," Lewis said.

The sheriff poured himself another drink.

"No great loss," he said. "She's better off without him. Good-looker, isn't she?"

"A very pleasant girl," Lewis said.

"I must go and see her now!" I said.

Lewis blinked.

The sheriff yawned.

"Ambulance'll be here soon," he said, apropos of nothing.

"Do you think you ought to, Saul?"

"I've got to," I said.

Lewis nodded.

"You want to break the news to her yourself?"

"Who's more qualified?" I said, putting a sad bitterness into my voice.

"Get your shoulder attended to first. Wait for the ambulance," the sheriff said. "No point in risking infection. I'll drive round there myself with you. Old Cromarty place, isn't it?"

Lewis said yes.

"Do you wish me to come with you, Saul?" he said.

"No, I think I'd rather not, Mr. Lewis. I'll get in touch with you later in the day."

"Very well," he said. "In that case I think I shall go home. Thank God you weren't hurt badly."

"Yeah," the sheriff said, "it was a near shave . . ."

An hour later, my arm in a sling and most of the pain gone from my shoulder, we drove out of the grounds and by way of the road reached the cottage where Anna lived.

The smoke from the chimney told us that Anna was already up.

I was afraid that Anna might give away the fact that I had already visited her since my arrival on the estate and was worried, since my companion was the sheriff himself, about the results of such a disclosure.

I need not have worried. As soon as Anna had opened the door and seen me in the company of the sheriff, she cried:—

"Saul!"

"Anna!" I said, moving forward and taking her in my arms. Then, pretending to rub my cheek against hers, I whispered: "This is the first time I've seen you since I arrived."

She told me she understood by a slight pressure on my arm.

"Sorry, sheriff, you understand," I said, "Anna was my governess and we haven't seen one another for many years."

The sheriff looked as though he was not the least interested. He was looking across toward the woods and was lighting another of his foul cigars. A moment later he turned.

"Better tell her at once," he said.

"Tell me what?" said Anna, her eyes widening with surprise.

"Anna, you must try to be strong . . . Inez is dead . . ."

Her face went white.

"Dead?"

"Mr. Folsrom shot your husband in self-defense," the sheriff interposed. And I thought he looked at her closely.

She stared from him to me and with a small cry she fainted. I caught her as she fell and carried her into the cottage. The sheriff—he was called McCabe—followed me in.

I carried her over to the bed and a moment later McCabe joined me with a glass of water.

"Good-looking broad," he said to me as he handed me the glass.

I nodded, and raising Anna on my arm, I forced the glass between her lips.

A moment later her eyes flickered open.

She stared at me.

I looked at McCabe.

He grinned. And then, when her gaze flitted to him, he became serious.

"Phone me later in the morning, Mr. Folsrom," he said, giving me his number. "I'll get along now. Be seeing you."

He nodded to Anna and went out.

Neither of us spoke until we heard the car start and drive away.

"*You* killed Inez!"

I stroked her hair.

"You murdered him!"

"In cold blood," I said. "I waited for him for three nights. He came this morning just before dawn. I shot him twice between the eyes."

"Oh God!"

I thought she was going to faint again but she took hold of herself.

"I told you I loved him!"

"You told me he had the power of the beast over you. I shot the beast."

She was looking at me as a rabbit watches a snake.

Something stirred in me. I knew that I must act now or not at all. Coldly, with calculation, I slapped her across the face.

It was no spurious act and it was geared to the moment only in the sense that I was now ready to act at every moment in accordance with a new attitude. She had loved Inez. I thought about that night after night as I waited to slay him.

She had loved me in a different way.

My act of slapping her across the face had the effect of annihilating the past, of reversing the relation between us. In the future, *she* would obey.

It was not what I wanted, not what I had intended, not the situation for which I had made a thousand preparations while I was separated from her, but I had come to realize clearly that it was the only effective way, at least for the moment, for she was not ready to be that woman of my imagination, and in reversing things in this way I was at least able to put things in suspension; I should not have lost irrevocably.

Her expression had changed.

The fear was still there but it had undergone a subtle modulation; it was no longer stark panic, and all hatred had gone from her eyes. It was as though she were waiting for me to act again.

Slowly, holding her gaze, I bared myself, and as I did so I felt the sluice of urgent blood move to hardness. I looked down and her gaze followed my own. When our eyes met again, I climbed onto the bed beside her. Kneeling there, slowly, an inch at a time, I brought it toward her face. She stared at it, her whole attention riveted upon it, and then suddenly, when it was no more than six inches from her, she let out a small whimper, enclosed it like a valuable object in both hands, and took it in her mouth. As she did so, her liquid eyes closed, and I felt the sensual doting movement of her little tongue.

She was breathing heavily.

I moved around into a more comfortable position, cradling her head between my thighs, and grasping her back in both hands I fed her against me.

A few moments later, I felt her hands move round and thrust my trousers down about my thighs, and then her hands were on my buttocks, gripping and relaxing, gripping and relaxing, until the white spume rose up in me and spilled over into her greedy mouth.

She moaned and swallowed avidly.

I allowed it to remain there until she had consumed every last drop and then, gently, I removed it from between her lips, buttoned myself, and sat on a chair next to the bed.

I lit a cigarette.

She was gazing at me, her lips slack and wet, a haunted expression in her dark eyes. One of her hands had moved down to her crotch and she gripped it as though it were burning her.

"Take your clothes off," I said.

She responded with a whimper of delight.

A few seconds later she lay naked before me, her heavy white thighs slackly apart, her knees trembling.

I leaned over from my chair and laid my hand at her sex.

Her buttocks tightened and her belly moved upward hotly against my hand. Once again she had closed her eyes.

Gently, I stroked her belly as I would have stroked a cat. She uttered a moan of pleasure. I slipped one finger into her and massaged her clitoris with my thumb. The sweat had gathered on her thighs like hoarfrost. I threw away my cigarette and reached for her left breast. I took the budding nipple between thumb and forefinger and squeezed, gently at first and then with increased pressure. Her white belly swung upward in a strong arc against my other hand bearing the glistening black hairs which downed the juncture of her thighs. Softly, I slipped a second finger into her.

She let out a small gasp of pleasure. Her whole torso seemed to radiate pleasure, a strange well-being born perhaps of the slow consciousness of being an instrument. I played with her then, the fingers of one hand running riotously about her body while the fingers of the other coaxed at her wet crevice until four of them were embedded up to the hilt.

She was delirious and the strange intensity of her desire imparted itself to me, causing me to harden for the second time. But I restrained myself. I turned her over, puncturing her again with four fingers, only this time, as I came from the rear, I moved suddenly and brutally into her anus with my thumb. Her moan exploded in a whinnying sound. Before it had ended, I brought my free hand, the palm flat and rigid, down with full force across her buttocks. She bucked madly and soundlessly, the sweat appearing in small pinheads on her back. I struck again, my mind suddenly overtaken by the scene of years ago when Uncle Harris had thrashed her with the riding whip. A new respect for him crept over me. I saw her again with the garter belt and the silk stockings, all the exciting tackle of her humiliation.

Quickly, I deserted her and walked across to the chest of drawers. In the top one I found what I was looking for, a black garter belt and dark nylon stockings. I carried them back across to her and threw them on the bed beside her.

She was quivering with lust.

Obediently, she slipped into the stockings and slung the garter belt around her creamy belly. From under the bed I took a pair of high-heeled shoes and laid them beside her. She put them on and lay down again on her back.

Slowly I leaned over her and smelled the heat of her body, and then, without further delay, I stripped naked and threw myself on top of her, my member sliding into her like a launched hull into a lake. My belly prised down on hers feeling the sleek line of the garter belt and my thighs brushed against hers to feel the smoothness of the flesh under the almost transparent nylon stockings. Still sunk deep in her, I closed her thighs within mine, imprisoning them, forbidding them movement, and then the nylon was against the soft inner surfaces of my thighs, titivating, informing me of her humiliating surrender. With my hands on her rump, I flicked the elastics of her garter belt against her smooth skin, rubbing at the same time with my front against these dainties which she had put on for my delight. My naked feet slipped into the insteps of her high-heeled shoes, and I had her thighs open against mine, incredibly soft, prising them down with my own, my muscles bulging, her shins clamped down under mine, the full roundness of her calves against the bed, and her feet levered outward by the pressure of my feet within the insteps of her shoes. Her whole torso was thus laced to mine and her hot dripping sex was nailed and split like a soft wound from which fluid flowed.

It was almost without movement then—the blood surging blindly within us—that we were carried together into delirium. A simple but urgent flexing of the buttocks, a hardening and softening of the muscles of the lower abdomen, and thus we rocked, one body welded to the other in lust, into oblivion.

She was streaming sweat when I rose from her, her whole body emitting the stench of woman, her muscles grown flaccid with exhaustion, and her consciousness dying into itself, into being.

I came away from her wet. Her sweat and my own mingled on my belly and flanks, and the sunrise new and warm streamed in the cottage window giving my feet a yellow luminescence.

Still naked, I moved over to the window and looked out. In the near distance the woods within which a few hours earlier I had destroyed this woman's husband were visible. I turned and gazed at her naked body spread out in lassitude on the bed. In that bed, a few moments before, I had destroyed him again.

"Anna . . ."

I had to repeat her name for a second time before her head fell round to look at me.

A strange and beautiful smile played on her full lips. Her right hand lay on her right breast, tenderly, the arm crooked at the elbow.

"Inez is dead," I said.

The smile did not leave her lips.

I walked over and stroked the loose hair back from her temple.

"You'll come to my home immediately after the inquest," I said.

Her soft black eyes flickered.

Her hand moved up and held mine where it was.

Chapter 6

*T*wo days later Lewis invited himself to dinner at my house. He phoned up toward midday and asked whether it would be convenient for him to come. I agreed at once, saying that I looked forward to seeing him again. But he was rather noncommittal on the telephone. He appeared to have something on his mind.

I went at once to the kitchen to tell Kirstin that I was expecting a guest for dinner. The kitchen was located in the basement next to the laundry. As I walked along the stone corridor I heard a queer noise which I took to be a girl's whimper. I hesitated and listened. The sound came again.

I walked quietly up to the kitchen door and knocked.

Inside there was a scuffling movement and then, almost at once, the door opened and Kirstin, a strange smile on her broad Nordic features, looked out at me. When she saw me she stepped back to allow me to enter.

Mona, the upstairs maid, left the kitchen by the back door as I entered. I was again struck by the exceeding whiteness of her skin under her rich chestnut red hair. Green eyes, I remembered—she was a pretty child.

"Did you wish something, sir?" Kirstin's voice was obsequious, perhaps amused at the same time. The sound of her voice aroused me from my own thoughts.

"Oh yes, Kirstin. I have a guest coming to dinner tonight, Mr. Lewis. That's all really."

I hesitated, looking at her.

She was a big-boned woman with heavy flesh who gave the impression, as I have remarked before, of being a masseuse or an abortionist or something of that nature. Her hair was pale blonde and her small blue eyes were sunk in her doughlike face like buttons in soft wax. Her features were rather fine in spite of the roll of fat under her chin. She was about five feet seven inches tall and in her high heels which she wore all the time must have stood about five feet nine or ten, two inches at the most shorter than myself.

"Very good, Mr. Folsrom," she said, but the expression on her face did not fit the words somehow and I found myself gazing at her without quite knowing why.

Her small blue eyes returned my stare almost impertinently, and then suddenly she turned and busied herself with her pots in which the lunch was being cooked.

"How's your shoulder, sir?" she said without turning around.

I looked at her back for a moment without replying. Her shoulders were broad and powerful, the buttocks heavily muscled, her bare calves under the white housecoat fat and smooth like codfish.

"Better, thanks, Kirstin. A bit stiff, that's all."

"Soon put that right," she said without looking at me. "A little massage is what you need, sir."

"Massage? You're not a masseuse by any chance, Kirstin?"

"I did a bit of it before I took up this work," she said. "If you like I'll give you a rub sometime during the afternoon, Mr. Folsrom."

I hesitated.

Was it my own wayward imagination which divined suggestion in her words?

"That's very good of you, Kirstin. Come up around four o'clock if that suits you."

"Very good, sir."

"I think a brace of pigeon for tonight, Kirstin."

"Yes, Mr. Folsrom."

I left the kitchen.

All during the afternoon the thought returned to me that there was something almost sinister about this big Swedish woman who was now the head of my household staff. What was it precisely? And why did I have a sense of strange expectation from her impending visit? And the whimper which I had most certainly heard on the way to the kitchen—what did that mean? My curiosity was aroused. I spent a reflective two hours after lunch was over . . .

Exactly at four o'clock Kirstin knocked at the door.

"Come in!"

She entered, dressed as always in her white housecoat.

She took in the furniture of the library at a glance.

"There's a divan in your dressing room, sir. I think that would be more suitable."

I nodded.

"All right. Let's go up."

At the foot of the stairs she paused to allow me to go up first.

"After you, Kirstin," I said.

She went up first and I followed.

In the dressing room she instructed me to remove my upper clothing. My wound was covered with sticking plaster and lint. She made me lie face downward on the divan, and, sitting sideways beside me, she laid her large hands on my back, the thumbs parallel with my spine. Slowly, and with firm pressure, she began to massage me. She had produced a bottle of oil from her housecoat pocket, so that the friction would not irritate my skin.

In a very few minutes I felt utterly relaxed. Her hands seemed to possess the power of magic, at once soothing and stimulating, caressing and threatening. I breathed heavily, partly because of the pressure she exerted and the resultant expulsion of air from my lungs and partly because her strong hands, imparting something of their mystery, had given birth to a crude sexual excitement in me.

She had massaged my whole back, from my neck and shoulders down to the waistband of my trousers.

"If you'll just push your trousers down a moment, sir, I'll finish you off properly," she said.

I assented without argument, doing as I was bid. And then her hands were at my buttocks and thighs, kneading the flesh like baker's dough and bringing relaxation to all the muscles of my legs.

There is an obvious metaphor: I was like clay in her hands. I think she could have done anything she wished to me at that moment. I couldn't remember ever having been so entirely in another's power. Even as a child, when Anna used me, she had to be coaxed and encouraged to take control. But at the moment I made the mental resolution that I should resist nothing Kirstin left off massaging me, took a towel, and rubbed me briskly from head to foot.

"I'm sure you feel better now, sir," she said, looking down at me from her small blue eyes. "You might take a bath, now."

"Yes, thanks, Kirstin," I said. "It's very good of you to have taken all this trouble."

"No trouble at all, sir. Keeps my hand in. But I must get back to the kitchen now if there's to be dinner tonight."

I nodded.

A moment later Kirstin and her wonderful hands were gone.

I walked over to the mirror and looked at myself. My face was flushed and my eyes were bright as though I had a fever. I turned away from my own image, an inarticulate shadow of dread stirring somewhere within me.

"The pigeon is excellent," Lewis said with a smile. "I'm glad at least you didn't dispense with Kirstin's services!"

"I doubt if I shall ever do that," I laughed, and as I said it a queer feeling of impotence swept over me. It was as though her hands touched me at that moment, firmly, purposively, moving muscles as though they were her own.

Suddenly Lewis became serious.

"By the way, Saul, I have a number of questions I should like to ask you. Do you mind?"

"Not at all, Mr. Lewis. I'll be only too glad to answer. There's nothing I'd like more than for us to understand one another."

"I'm glad to hear it, my boy! I won't beat about the bush."

"Fire ahead," I replied, helping myself to some green peas. "More wine?"

"No thank you, Saul, I have to watch nowadays! A little every day and not too much at a time."

"Gather ye rosebuds!" I said.

"Tell me, Saul," Lewis said, becoming serious once again, "tell me why you shot Inez twice . . ."

I was slightly taken aback by the question. When I looked at him I saw he was watching me closely, ready to weigh my answer.

I shrugged my shoulders.

"Well, I don't know, really . . . there he was . . . taking a pot at me . . . I didn't really stop to think. The triggers were together. I fired them both, right, left, like that, automatically . . ."

"I see," Lewis said.

"Why do you ask?"

When he didn't reply, I said: "You're not suggesting I killed him on purpose?"

He was looking at me seriously. He did not reply to my question.

"My God! I didn't even know Inez! And apart from that, it was too dark and it happened too suddenly for me to see who it was at the time!"

"You're quite sure of that?"

"Of course I am! What on earth makes you think otherwise?"

Lewis leaned forward.

"Three days before you shot Inez, Saul, you visited Anna. After you shot Inez, you pretended you hadn't seen her since your return. I want you to think before you reply. The inquest is in a few days and some of these facts may come out."

I nodded. I was wondering just how much he knew.

"First of all, tell me how you know I visited Anna," I said.

"What does it matter?" he said quietly. "You were seen leaving the cottage. You had a horse with you . . ."

"Yes, well it seems that's known," I said in a tired voice.

"Do you see what I'm getting at, Saul?"

"No, I'm damned if I do!" I lied.

"It's just possible that you arranged this killing between you as you did the other, don't you see?"

"Good God! How fantastic! What possible motive could we have had? You can't think that!"

"I don't know what to think, Saul. I want *you* to tell *me*. For example, why did you lie about having seen her?"

I laughed bitterly.

"At first it was simply a desire not to displease you! I knew how you felt about it. And then when I'd committed myself, I couldn't go back on it . . . remember, I had just killed a man. I was scared. I didn't want to put any stupid ideas into people's heads. I see now I did wrong to hide the fact."

"You certainly did! If the sheriff hears about this he may become suspicious."

"Not if he doesn't know about the other," I said.

Lewis was looking at me sternly.

"Saul, I must be convinced in my own mind of your innocence."

I made an impatient gesture.

"How can I possibly convince you? You appear to jump to a great many conclusions for a man of your experience and intelligence!"

"I jump to no conclusions!" Lewis snapped. "I simply wish to ascertain the facts. I shall ask you another question. Did you make love to Anna when you rode over to see her?"

He had caught me off my guard. That was the last question I expected. When I hesitated, I decided I would have to admit it.

"Yes. I made love to her."

"Thank you at least for being honest," he said. "Now, in the light of this, do you think the sheriff is still without a case?"

"Does McCabe know?"

"That's not the point!" Lewis said sternly. "It is I who must be satisfied."

"Before I answer any further questions, Mr. Lewis," I said coldly, "I'd like to ask you a question."

He nodded almost imperceptibly.

"Are you my friend or my enemy?"

He raised his eyebrows.

"Are there no conditions to friendship?"

"Certainly there shouldn't be if I'm polite enough to

answer your questions!" I said. "Normally in an affair like this I should consult my lawyer before I made any statement whatsoever. And I certainly shall answer no more questions until I have your assurance on this point."

"Yes," he said at last. "I suppose that is justified."

"I should think it is." I replied calmly. "I shouldn't have dreamt of answering your questions had I not taken your friendship for granted."

When he dropped his eyes to the table I realized I had touched him at his weakest point; I had appealed to his sense of honor.

What an advantage I had over him!

"I can only say this," I went on in a calm voice, "I give you my assurance on two points. On my honor, I shot in self-defense, and I hadn't the slightest idea at whom I was shooting. I can't say more."

He made a tired gesture with his right hand. It was a gesture of defeat.

When he spoke next it was to say: "Thank you, Saul. That's really all I wanted to know. I shall respect your confidence. I was simply troubled in my own mind about you. I'm sorry."

"Forget it, Mr. Lewis, I'm just sorry we didn't have this talk immediately after it happened."

He nodded.

"Tell me one thing more," he said suddenly. "What do you intend to do about Anna? I hope you aren't thinking of persuading her to remain in the neighborhood?"

"I honestly don't know, sir. Sometimes I think I owe it to her to marry her and at other times I think it would be better if she went."

"Much better, Saul. Take my word for it! You should not even contemplate keeping her here."

"Anyway, I must wait till after the inquest! Who knows, they may charge me with murder . . ."

I shook my head in a way which implied: what a ridiculous situation!

"No, I don't think so," Lewis said. "The man had an evil reputation. He is no loss to the community."

"Poor Inez!" I said.

He brightened when I said that.

"I'm glad you said that, Saul," he said. "It makes me feel much better. I think I could even manage some of this cheese!"

I laughed.

"Help yourself," I said.

He looked up, blinking through his spectacles.

"Pearson, the junior in your late uncle's firm, is going to call on you. He will be at the inquest with you. I should tell him as much as possible if I were you. He will advise you what statement to make before the coroner."

I smiled as I watched him cut a liberal slice of Munster cheese . . .

After Lewis had gone I remained in the library until shortly after midnight. Lewis' curiosity as to my motives and behavior was rather disturbing. If he persisted in taking this kind of interest in my affairs, sooner or later he would surely discover something which he would feel bound to reveal to the authorities. Thus, although I had no particular plan of action in mind, I made a mental note that it would be necessary to find a way either of making him give up interest in me or of shutting his mouth.

His death, of course, would have solved the problem admirably, but any move on my part to hasten that death would be perilously made; apart from the risk of murder itself, I had no means of knowing what written records he would leave behind him, a package of papers perhaps in some bank vault, marked "To be opened in the event of my sudden death . . ." He was a shrewd man, and dangerous because he was an idealist.

As no immediate solution presented itself, I decided to go to bed, but on the way up I had a sudden desire to visit the old wing of the house which to my knowledge had not been used since I left as a child-murderer for England. Perhaps I would install Anna there after the inquest: the whole wing could be renovated and turned into a large apartment for her.

Thus, on the first landing, I turned right and walked along the passage which led to the old wing.

As I came to the end of the connecting corridor, I was surprised by a slit of light which appeared under one of the doors toward the end of the old wing corridor. It was all the more startling as the passage itself was in pitch darkness.

I came to a dead stop and listened. Vague noises came to me where I stood, but they were muffled, almost inaudible, and only served to deepen the mystery.

The light and the sounds came from the room which had formerly been Anna's.

And then suddenly I remembered the bathroom

through whose keyhole I had witnessed the strange sexual scene of Anna being taken by my uncle. With a growing sense of excitement I moved silently along the corridor toward the glimmer from the window at the end and when I came to the bathroom I opened the door silently and went in. A slit of light came from under the door of the adjoining bedroom. As I sank to my knees at the key-hole I had an overpowering premonition that Kirstin would be involved in the mystery. There was something about Kirstin, a quality at once repulsive and attractive, which made me suspect that in some strange way she would be involved in my own destiny . . .

❧

It is almost impossible to describe the scene to which I was the unknown witness.

The horror of it, its sticky insectal attraction, its obscenity, the salaciousness, the ruttish lewdness of the actions and of those who took part, the black sanctity of the setting—later, as we shall see, to be improved—the balletlike movements of the participants each of whom in every erotic gesture participated religiously, blasphe-mously, but without a suggestion of mockery, the weird radiance of the paints used on white willing flesh, the helpless, doting abjectness of the two maids and the cruel and scandalous beauty of the priestess, Kirstin,— all this transported the ceremony out of the realm of the common orgy, lending it solemnity, the solemnity of what is dangerous and deadly, for blood was to be shed, and the three grey rats cowering in the corner near a hunk of red beef twitched in fear and trembling as the ceremony advanced.

All furniture had been removed, since when I had no idea. All the filth and rubbish imaginable had been spread about the floor. Straw, excrement, rotten wood, kitchen waste, numberless things without identity, and the grey skeletons of three human beings.

The walls had been splashed with some kind of black paint, splotched here and there with red and what looked like sheep's wool. The sight and odor of the setting were obnoxious.

Kirstin was standing stark naked, her feet apart and her hands on her broad hips, like a piece of neo-realist sculpture.

It was perhaps the most powerful female torso I had ever laid eyes on. From her thick neck under her melonish blonde head the muscles swept down across her chest to the pale round moons of her breasts, each stuck with a nipple the size of a large black grape and tattooed to look like enormous hairy spiders. The illusion was magnificent. It was as though two spiders clung there drawing blood, their bloated bodies hard with suck. Below, across the sweep of her teeming white belly, a perfect web was marked, spotted here and there with red, and at her navel another spider clung, grosser, hairier than the others, looking down the sweeping web to the dark and hairy center at her crotch. Thus her whole muscled front, the thick slabs of the thighs, the great, creamy, hunky abdomen, the hips, supported the web of which the center was the black hole of her sex and upon which crawled three terrible spiders.

Her large white toes flexed themselves amongst the muck and she gazed downward at the two naked girls who sat on the floor, with their backs toward me, cross-legged, facing her.

The girls, of course, were Milly and Mona, as I was able to tell from their hair, the tresses of one dark, the tresses of the other chestnut red, cascading down over their pale white shoulder blades from which, shockingly, folds of cellophane were draped, and now, as I looked closer, I was able to see exactly what they were: between their slim white arms and the sides of their torsos, much like the webbing of a duck's feet, artificial cellophane wings had been stuck with adhesive tape, so that when their arms moved the wings did also, like the wings of insects.

I watched, fascinated.

Kirstin was talking quietly and the girls, cross-legged amongst the muck, were seated submissively on their soft young haunches, nodding their pretty heads in comprehension.

Then Kirstin broke her pose and moved backward to the far corner of the room, still facing me. A bench had been placed diagonally across the corner, one end touching each of the walls.

Kirstin now climbed upon this and stood, her thick legs wide apart and her plump white arms spread wide and high in crucifixion.

I stared in horror.

She was strung across the corner of the room like an ugly web of black spiders.

She spoke.

At once the girls got up and moved naked about the room, fluttering their translucent wings. Each time they neared the corner where the rats were the rats bared their teeth and the hair rose in coarse, quivering spines at the backs of their necks. It was only as the girls moved that I noticed Milly's belly was shaded a bottle blue, and that Mona's was striped yellow and black, tawny as a wasp. I glanced at Kirstin. She was speaking again.

Each girl picked up a skeleton. The fantasy began. I was conscious at once of the fact that fixed firmly on each skeleton was a rubber penis. Carefully, in a practiced way, each girl slipped it into her, draped the arms of a skeleton over her back and shoulders, and laid herself down on the filthy straw. To see a skeleton pricking a young girl, the bones bouncing like a beaded parrot-cage on her soft belly, is a strange sight. It did not last long. I had the impression that Kirstin was impatient for her little insects to become stuck in her web. She said something and the girls rose immediately, allowing the skeletons to tumble onto the floor. They began to fly again, or rather, to make the motions of flying. Mona was more graceful than Milly. Her movements were less abrupt and the flesh of her buttocks was a startling white against her red hair.

I was trembling with the pleasure of anticipation. By this time, no doubt remained in my mind that soon I should be taking part in these intimate ceremonies. I saw at last in Kirstin the woman to whom I could become committed.

Anna? There was no need to lose Anna now. She belonged to me, but belonging to me as she did, I would never be able to have that from her which I had desired from the beginning.

But these thoughts were soon pushed from my mind by the pressure of what was going on in front of my eyes.

Mona had arrived in front of Kirstin and was fluttering her wings as though attracted by the web. It was most lifelike, although she was more like a moth blinded by light than a wasp about to be trapped in a spider's web.

Kirstin's small blue eyes watched her closely. I held my breath. Mona now ran against Kirstin's powerful belly, rubbing her cheek there, and Kirstin's arms descended like claws, which in fact they were, for she was wearing some kind of points on her fingers, thimbles, perhaps, with metal points, and the cellophane wings were torn away from the pretty shoulder blades and blood trickled from scratches on Mona's white back. She was falling now to her knees, a frail insect beaten to death by another more powerful, and her hovering lips came suddenly to rest at the dead center of the web, on the black mass of Kirstin's powerful sex. Kirstin's talons at once grasped the fair child by the hair, forcing the young, tear-stained face into the dark night of her thighs, and then Kirstin was down on top of the girl, the girl helpless on the straw, her head held firmly between Kirstin's massive thighs.

Milly, meanwhile, continued to flutter about the room, but soon she too came within Kirstin's reach, reeling almost drunkenly, and was suddenly caught by the ankle and dragged off her feet into such a position that Kirstin was able to suck at her sex, avidly, and with great moans and breathing. The three women now thrashed about on the filthy straw, and Milly's mouth crept slowly toward Mona's sex and soon the perfect rope of women's bodies was formed, a circle of frantic limbs, three mouths embedded at three sexes, and a dull dunting of flesh. Both girls were bleeding freely from the scratches inflicted by Kirstin's steel claws; and then, Kirstin, with terrible power, had freed herself from the triple embrace and crushed the two young things under her huge body, rubbing, rubbing voluptuously against the bleeding flesh.

The rats, meanwhile, had begun to nibble at the meat . . .

§§

It was at this point that I came away. I had no curiosity to see any more. I was far more concerned with the possibility of meeting Kirstin on another plane than that of master and servant. I paced about the library consumed with a mad passion to call her at once and throw myself at her feet.

Here at last was the risk which I was looking for, the intensity, the obscenity, the criminality to which I could bring the willing consent of my own body and soul. The vision of Anna paled before the image of Kirstin. The one wished nothing more than to be a victim; the other would dare to victimize. What hellish green fires must have burned within Kirstin to make the woman-beast of her that I saw in action!

I had to make a compact at once. I would wait an hour when the orgy surely would be over and then I would ring for her. For the first time in my life I had met a woman to whom I could dedicate myself. The old craving to be the instrument of another's will surged up in me anew. Kirstin. Kirstin. Faust is waiting for you . . .

At one thirty A.M. I rang for her.

Seven minutes later she knocked at the door of the library.

"Come in!"

Kirstin, dressed as usual in her white housecoat, entered.

She looked at me curiously.

"You rang for me, Mr. Folsrom?"

"Yes, Kirstin. Come in please and sit down."

With a shrug of her broad shoulders she did as I asked.

"Something to drink?"

"I'll take a small whiskey," she said.

I poured it for her and carried it across to her where she sat. Her eyes flickered as I handed it to her.

I was rather nervous. I still didn't know how to begin.

"You're from Stockholm, Kirstin?"

"No. From Kiruna."

"That's in the North?"

She nodded. There was a suggestion of impatience in her eyes.

"You strike me as a very strong character, Kirstin."

She shrugged and drained her glass.

"Was this what you called me for, Mr. Folsrom. It's very late and I'm tired. I have to get up early in the morning."

"Not necessarily. I could excuse you from your duties."

"How do you mean?"

"Perhaps I could use you in another capacity, one that would be more profitable for you."

"So?"

"I thought it best to wait until all the other servants were in bed. I didn't wish us to be disturbed. Make yourself comfortable and help yourself to more whiskey." I passed her the bottle from which she poured herself another drink, this time more liberally.

"What's on your mind, Mr. Folsrom?"

"I'm thinking of a spider-woman," I said casually.

She flushed.

"Spider-woman? I don't know what you mean. What is a spider-woman?"

I was gazing at her big calves. Her legs were crossed at the knees.

"Would you mind uncrossing your legs, Kirstin?"

She did so slowly, watching me suspiciously.

"If I were to lie down on the floor and kiss your feet, Kirstin, what would you do?"

She didn't reply. A queer light played in her eyes.

Slowly, cautiously, I went to my knees, and then, lying supine on the floor, I raised one of her fat white feet to my lips.

She laughed harshly.

"So that's what you want!" she said.

She stood up and removed her white housecoat. She lifted the skirt of her nightdress high above her smooth white belly, exhibiting the dark maw of her sex and the hairy spider of her navel.

"Get up," she said. "On your knees! Look at it!"

The huge chunky thighs were as white as chalk, anastomosed by the black tendrils of the web.

She hitched the front part of her skirt above her waist and sat down on the edge of an armchair. Her big fingers opened the lips of her vagina, exhibiting the orchidaceous flesh, pink, oily, obscene.

"Touch that," she said huskily, "and you won't get away again . . ."

I gazed from the flower to the spider. The craving ran like a plague through my body.

"Your lips," she said. "Like you were praying . . ."

I lunged forward.

My mouth hit her soft crotch with the force of a fist . . .

Chapter 7

*T*he inquest went very smoothly. The verdict was "Death by Misadventure."

The coroner in his final speech extended his sympathy both to myself and to Anna, who had come to court in black widow's clothes.

Lewis was present. He seemed preoccupied. I had the impression that all his old distrust of me had returned. That worried me, and yet I knew that, for the moment at least, he would not betray me.

"I am giving up my trusteeship of your uncle's estate," he said when the inquest was over. "I have nominated Pearson to take my place and the other trustees have raised no objections. I'm sorry Saul, but as long as these horrible doubts remain in my mind—and I'm afraid I can't get rid of them, I'm getting old, I suppose—I don't feel able to undertake the responsibilities of a trustee."

"You mean you still think I murdered Inez?"

"I don't know what to think, Saul. No . . . I don't honestly think I believe that, but Anna tells me now that you have invited her to live at your house and that she has accepted. I must say that under the circumstances I think that is frightful, most improper, and I suppose that is the reason for my decision. You must go your own way. And as I disapprove so heartily of your behavior in this business, I feel it would be better for both of us if we had nothing more to do with one another. I feel uncomfortable in your presence. I just do not know what to think of you. One moment I think you are a fine, lovable young man, and the next moment I think you are the epitome of evil, cold, calculating, utterly unscrupulous. I think I am even a little afraid of you. But there it is. I've told you my reasons."

He removed his spectacles and dabbed his eyes with a white handkerchief.

"I'm sorry you feel like that about it, Mr. Lewis. You must remember that Anna was very close to me once and I feel bound to look after her now. It's not money she needs. That would be easy. It is companionship. The knowledge that she is among people who love her. I'm sorry you can't understand."

He had put on his glasses again.

"I understand, Saul, that she is even now your mistress. I find that troubling, and, in light of what has happened, most shocking!"

"If you were a younger man, and if I didn't respect you as I do, Mr. Lewis, I should call you a prude. Does it not occur to you that the sexual act can be beautiful, even utterly spiritual?"

"Perhaps it can be for people who are in love with one another. Are you in love with Anna?"

"Yes."

"You don't say it with much conviction."

"You have romantic notions about love, Mr. Lewis. You consider it to be a kind of pit one falls into. I don't.

For me it is something that is chosen; something which is chosen and chosen again. It's the doing. Loving is making love, or caressing, or caring for. It's a practical act. We create it in choice and in act . . ."

"Come, I don't wish to discuss it, Saul," Lewis said quite coldly. "If you seriously love Anna, marry her, then perhaps one day I shall grow to see things your way. But for the moment, good-bye, and good luck."

We shook hands and I watched him move on his crutches toward his waiting car.

❧

Marry Anna?

Of course, that was impossible now. I was no longer a free agent. In a few days, Kirstin had made me the doting slave of her body and her will. Kirstin now slept with me every night, or rather, I slept with her, for it was she who had become pre-eminent and it was I who nightly slept with my head between the damp wet weight of her thighs. It was she who insisted upon this, and I loved and worshiped her for it, deriving more pleasure from my utter abasement than I had ever drawn from that of another. I trusted Kirstin's skill and ability to bring me gradually to the supreme joys of suffering. How interesting all this was, for she knew what to do down to the last detail, by a strange twisted intuition, and I had the intelligence and the imagination to savor every subtlety of her cruel female will. I worshiped her for the subtlety almost as much as I worshiped her for the gross, hairy sex into which, nightly, I died . . .

I must now speak at length about this strange relation which was to lead slowly but surely to the utter domination of my will by hers, to the extinction of the being, Saul.

It was very gradual, that is to say, in the sense that she never hurried things, that she never forced upon me more pain or indignity than I could bear. The coercion was subtle, accepted, desired positively, entered into with religious fervor. I was seldom required to do anything which I had not already chosen to do in imagination, and she was patient as she insisted, insinuating, corrupting, polluting, humiliating so that hour by hour my love grew more and more monstrous and my servility more complete.

That first night she had drawn my lips away again, her strong fingers hard and clutching in my hair. "Lick it," she said. "You're like a little pig!" And I was, and that was precisely what she wanted me to be, and so she told me I was, and so I was . . .

"I'm taking you to bed," she said. "I want to talk all this over with you."

I followed her obediently to her own room.

"Strip!"

She sat fully dressed in her armchair and rapped out the command at me.

I hesitated and then took off all my clothes. I stood naked before her. I had a painful erection.

"Come here!"

I walked across to her.

She took the whole knot of my vitals into her large hands, caressing, squeezing slightly.

"Get into bed. Under the covers."

I did so.

A moment later, naked except for black silk stockings and a black garter belt which she had put on, she joined me in the bed and switched out the light.

"Easier this way the first night," she said.

A moment later she moved me downward so that I lay diagonally across the bed, my head between her thighs. The soft flesh radiated warmth and wetness at my face. "There's your pigsty," she whispered, caressing my neck with her fingers.

In the utter darkness I gave fiercely in to my desire. I licked deeper and deeper, mixing my saliva with her slime, and the hot viscous substance spread over my eyes and my chin like a soft cloud. It was sticky, salty, and sweet at the same time. A short while later, her powerful buttocks quivered and her odor enveloped me completely.

The following night we were standing naked in her room. She took me in her arms and kissed me on the lips. "You'll do strange things for me, my darling!" she said.

Later, under the covers, my head lost in ecstasy at her sweating crotch, I felt a sudden, sickening, acrid trickle at my lips. I closed them sharply and shut my eyes. A moment later, the warm stale liquid fell like a skin across my face and neck. When I felt the pressure of her thighs, I gave in and relaxed. It was a long time before, in the pungent heat, I fell into sleep.

In the morning she lay like a white stain on top of the red quilt, for the bed was wet and uncomfortable. "Down on me . . ." she whispered.

During the day she ran the house efficiently and in

company, either servants or guests, she accorded me all the respect due to the master of the house. But as soon as we were alone, her attitude changed: she would confide in me, invite me to confide in her, and make me do innumerable menial tasks for her. In the future, I was to wash her crotch for her at all times and with the dirty water I was to wash my face. I did so enthusiastically for her crotch was my God and I considered myself lucky to have the opportunity to wash my face in the water soiled by her crotch. As for my own vitals, I was to wash them at all times in her urine. I felt this was only as it should be, for after all, my sex was her dedicated slave. I was obliged to go with her each time she visited the lavatory. On those occasions, I would have the choice either of lying on the floor with my face under her feet or of resting my chin on the edge of the pan between her thighs with my forehead pressed against her belly. Both actions, she explained, helped her to vacate more easily. But I had to remember, she went on to say, that she would not always explain things, that she did so only to show me that she was worthy of trust, in the beginning, but not for long, for there were many things she would require of me, and certainly many of them would be quite unreasonable. Many, many menial little tasks, each calculated to intensify my abasement, to prostrate my spirit before her powerful will. I was amazed at her genius for taking control. I loved her more frantically with each subsequent groveling act she required of me.

On the morning of the inquest, she gave me her soiled knickers. "Keep these," she said. "You'd better buy me two dozen pairs of nylon ones when you're in town today. You must keep my soiled panties from now on."

I put them in a safe place like a dog burying his bone.

"This Anna," she said. "I've seen her in town, I think. I want her. Be sure to bring her back for me . . ."

Marry Anna?

Of course, that was impossible now . . .

❧

When Lewis had gone I joined Anna where she waited for me in my car. Cliff closed the door behind me.

"The old Cromarty cottage," I said.

We drove in silence into the country. I took Anna's hand. She hesitated to allow me to keep it. She frowned in Cliff's direction.

"Don't worry about Cliff," I said in a voice loud enough for him to hear and his head nodded imperceptibly.

Anna relaxed.

"Thank God that's all over," she sighed.

I leaned over and kissed her on the lips. At the same time, my hand moved under her skirt, and slipped under her panties to her sex. I stroked the beautiful, soft, hairy thing for her and she rubbed against me like a cat. I took her on my knee and played with her, and then, slipping my member out I allowed it to burst in at the side of her nylon panties into the hot little cauldron of her sex. She moaned and hid her face against my neck. I relaxed in my seat and eased my power into the voluptuous warm weight. The joggling of the car on the rough road up toward her cottage was enough to bring my sliding ecstasy to her womb.

She packed two bags and rejoined me in the car.

Ten minutes later we entered the front door of my house.

Mona showed her to her room.

I went into the library and sent for Cliff.

He entered obsequiously.

"What do I pay you, Cliff?"

"Forty bucks plus keep," he answered at once.

"We'll make it sixty," I said.

He grinned. "Thanks a lot, Mr. Folsrom. If there's anything I can do at any time . . ."

"Thanks, Cliff. I'll remember."

He went out.

A moment later Kirstin came in.

"You got to make her do things, you understand?"

I nodded.

"And then one day you tell her I want her and that's that, see?"

"Yes."

She smiled at me.

"You can kiss it," she said.

I fell to my knees as she moved forward, raising her skirt.

Things were moving quickly.

"You can have Milly," Kirstin said one day to me. "Go and take her now in the bedroom. She's waiting for you."

I went at once.

I threw her naked onto the bed, prised open her

plump little thighs, and stuck her at once. I rode her roughly to my climax and made her lick me afterward. She was still lying naked on the bed when I left.

"Good for you," Kirstin said to me later in the day. "I liked the way you handled Milly."

Anna was not difficult to handle.

Had I not had the benefit of seeing a genius at work? Gradually, I subdued her. When we slept together, she slept with her head between my thighs. I simply reversed the procedures Kirstin used on me.

Within a week, I led her naked and quivering to Kirstin's bedroom. Kirstin rose naked from her bed and felt Anna all over.

"Put some stockings and high heels on her first, and then let's see you whip her," Kirstin said.

She sat and watched.

I made Anna stand as she had stood for my uncle and I slashed her ten times on the naked buttocks with my riding crop.

"That's enough," Kirstin said. "Now get out and leave this hot bitch to me," she commanded. "Mona's waiting for you in her own bedroom. Go to her . . ."

I moved out like a willing hound.

As I did so I heard the smack of one fleshy body against another.

Mona met me on her knees, her green eyes shining, her pale shoulders curving forward as her arms encircled my buttocks to take my rampant lust in her mouth . . .

Chapter 8

*N*ow that old Lewis is no longer a trustee you should be able to get more money," Kirstin said one day.

"I'll try at once," I said.

"For two thousand dollars we can renovate the cellars," she said. "I want to get some implements. I've decided the women must be branded."

"I'll get the money."

"And we need some more servants," she said. "I'm interviewing some girls tomorrow. I'll take another maid at once and another to start in two weeks' time. It's easier if they come one at a time."

I nodded.

❧

Pearson proved quite intractable.

"I'm sorry, Saul," he said, dabbing his sleek black moustache with his forefinger, "but Mr. Lewis advised me before he handed over to me that I shouldn't raise your income at present. And really, I don't see any necessity for it. It was your late uncle's wish that you shouldn't come into the estate until the age of thirty. I think it's only right that we should respect his wishes."

"Is that final?"

"For the moment at least, yes."

"If I speak to the other trustees?"

"I shouldn't think they'd be very cooperative, Saul. They have always allowed Mr. Lewis to do pretty much as he saw fit. I don't think they would be against me in this matter."

"Very well," I said.

Lewis again! The man seemed to dog my tracks, to put every difficulty in my way. What business was it of the old fool's! Why couldn't he leave me alone?

Later in the afternoon I went for a ride. I left the estate and cantered across the countryside.

About four o'clock I caught a glimpse of another rider, a slim blonde girl on a grey gelding. I urged my mare forward to overtake her. After a mock race we came to a halt close together, breathing heavily and laughing.

The girl was beautiful with superbly slanted grey-green eyes, long smoke-blonde hair, and a perfect figure which even her riding clothes couldn't conceal.

"Where are you from?" I said with a laugh.

"I'm staying with my uncle for a couple of weeks," she replied. "Mr. Lewis. Perhaps you know him?"

My brow darkened.

"Lewis? So you're Lewis' niece?"

"Yes, why? What's wrong with that?"

"I'm Saul Folsrom," I said, watching her closely for a reaction.

"Oh!"

She was flushed now and seemed at a loss for words.

"You must have heard about me from your uncle. What did he say about me?"

"Nothing really, Mr. Folsrom," she said, recovering her poise. "He wrote of you, you see, some time ago when you first decided to return from England. He suggested that when I came to visit him he should at least be able to introduce me to a companion of my own age. You were coming back, you see?"

I nodded and held my horse in check. "Go on . . . please . . ."

She smiled and then became serious again.

"Well, when I arrived two days ago and asked about you, he said he felt it would be better if we didn't meet. He didn't seem to want to talk about it, so naturally I let the matter drop. But I made a few inquiries and found out about the accident . . ."

"Yes?"

"And so I brought up the subject again with Uncle."

"And he told you he suspected me of being a murderer?"

"A murderer! No, he didn't say that! He simply said you were now living with the wife of the dead man and that he disapproved entirely of your behavior."

"Living with her?"

"That's what he said. Isn't it true?"

There was faint mockery in her lovely eyes.

"She's at my place. It was the least I could do. She's a lonely woman. No friend in the world apart from myself. She was my governess at one time. Perhaps your uncle told you?"

"Yes he said something like that, I remember . . ."

I changed the subject.

"Look," I said lightly, "why don't we ride together to the 'Morden' . . . that's a hotel country-club sort of place. We could have a drink and a chat there. I don't see why we shouldn't know one another. God, there's few enough people in the neighborhood worth knowing!"

She hesitated.

"It's getting late," she said. "It must be after four now. I'm driving with my uncle to dinner at Montpelier tonight. He wants me to be ready to leave about six-thirty."

"We can still make it," I replied. "If you ride back after five, you'll have ample time . . ."

"You don't know women!" she laughed. "I have to have a shower and then dress!"

"No more arguments!" I said jocularly, and spurred my mare forward. "Come on! You follow me!"

She laughed and followed.

"All right, I'm coming!" she said as she came alongside, "but don't tell anyone. I don't want my uncle to know!"

"Of course not!" I said with a laugh, and we cantered away toward the hotel.

"Yes, my uncle told me something about that," Vivian said with a slight frown. "I think it's horrible for you. I told him so. To have all that money and not to be able to touch it until you're thirty!"

I told her about my visit to Pearson in the early afternoon.

"He blamed it on your uncle, but he feels the same way himself. If only Uncle Harris had known me better, he wouldn't have put that ridiculous clause in the will!"

"But he died when you were young, didn't he?"

"Yes, worse luck."

"My father died when I was young too," Vivian said. "But fortunately I came into my money at twenty-one . . . two months ago now! It's good to be young and rich as well!"

I looked at her with a new interest.

"Your father was Lewis' brother?"

"No. His cousin. Mr. Lewis is not really my uncle though I've always thought of him as my uncle."

"You must be the heir to Lewis' property too, then?"

She laughed.

"Yes. That's why he likes me to be here. He hopes I'll give up living in Boston and come to settle down in Vermont."

She finished her dry Martini.

"Another?"

She nodded with a laugh.

I ordered two more dry Martinis.

"You know, Saul," she said, "I think that's why he wrote to me about you. Your uncle was his best friend. I think he hoped we might fall for one another!"

"It's not impossible, is it?"

She flushed.

"No, I don't suppose it is," she said seriously. "But he's dead against it now, because of this woman, Anna, I suppose."

Vivian was really one of the loveliest girls I had ever

seen. She drank her second Martini quickly and looked at her watch.

"I must fly!" she said.

I didn't try to detain her.

I rode part of the way with her.

"When shall I see you again?"

"Whenever you want to, of course," she said.

"I'll meet you tomorrow afternoon, same time, same place," I said.

"Till tomorrow," she said, and urging her horse forward, she cantered away from me without looking back. I watched her slim figure with the sleek blonde hair caught in a ponytail at the back of her head until it was out of sight. Then I turned aside and rode back to the estate.

"You say she's rich?"

Kirstin sat opposite me in the library, watching me carefully.

"Very rich, I suspect."

She got up and poured herself a drink. Then she sat down again, appeared to concentrate for a moment, and said: "How would you feel about marrying her, Saul?"

"Marry her!" I laughed. "That's impossible, you know that, Kirstin."

"Nothing is impossible," Kirstin said, "and this is not even improbable."

She threw me a taunting glance.

"In the first place you say she is a young Diana. I like that! A beautiful young woman, a woman of culture and refinement—that's more than we can say for what we've got already, ha! ha! I was down in the cellars an hour ago. They're all settling down quite nicely. The heat from the boiler room is sufficient for the moment. Well, get back to your beautiful Vivian! Are you falling in love with her, Saul?"

I flushed.

"Don't worry about that!" Kirstin said. "Go ahead! Fall in love with her! Bring her back here! You'll soon tire of her. You can work on her slowly, and then, when you think she's ready, we can show her the others. They're happy enough, God knows! All belly, breasts, and thighs. Sleep, eat, and fuck—that's what they like, no problems!"

"I couldn't bring her here!"

"Why not? You'll do as you're told, Saul. Don't forget that. Come here." Her voice was gentle. "Down," she said, "down, there's a good boy, ah! that's better . . ."

Her soft sex came against my face, her thighs brushing my cheeks.

"Now, listen to me!" she said. "The second point is that she's got money. We can use that, especially after what Pearson said. And there's a third point. Did it not occur to you? Lewis will be helpless. He won't be able to let out the secret about your uncle—she's all he's got in the world, this Vivian! We'll be good to her, Saul, and when she gets used to it, she'll help us of her own free will. And when you're married to his little Vivian, Lewis will soon see about freeing some of your money. Don't worry about that! He'll think that's the only way he can prevent you from spending hers! Now, how does it sound, Saul?"

Her strong hands massaged my shoulder muscles.

"Come down to the cellar, Saul. I want to show you the meat. Why don't you go in and have a good time with them? Take your riding crop. Keep them up to the mark!"

She led me down the stairs to the cellars. We passed those which contained coal and other junk and came at last to the huge cellar to which the light of day never penetrated. It was circular in shape, of a radius of about ten yards, so that the actual area covered by the floor was quite considerable. She slid back the small grill on the iron-studded door.

"Look at them, Saul! Aren't they beautiful? Not like the bitches that walk the street!"

The floor was covered with clean straw and for the moment the only light was that cast by the naked electric bulb suspended from the domelike ceiling.

The three women, naked, their soft haunches at rest, were sleeping, curled up like kittens together near the far wall. Beside them was a trough of food and a trough of clean spring water. On the other side was an open lavatory bowl and what the French call a *bidet*. Nothing else. A few chains dangled from the stone walls, and that was all.

"The new maid arrives tomorrow," Kirstin said. "I've given Mona her instructions. She's completely with us. I show her a few kindnesses, you know. She is our spy down here, just in case anything should go wrong. Not that I think it will. They've all got exactly what they want. Food, water, and good clean straw to sleep on. What more could a girl ask for, eh, Saul?"

I kissed her on the lips.

She reached down and took out my member, caressing it.

"I'm going to bring Mona upstairs tomorrow to corrupt the new maid. She has two weeks to do it. Meanwhile, take your clothes off and go and enjoy them. They're all yours . . . they always will be, Saul . . . as long as you're mine . . ."

She waited while I undressed in the boiler room and then she handed me the riding crop.

"Go in and separate them with that," she said with a laugh. "One good stroke each across those pretty buttocks of theirs! I'll lock the door behind you. I'll come back and let you out in an hour."

I nodded and went in, my rampant member swinging like a small cannon in front of me. She closed the door quietly behind me and turned the key in the lock.

I crossed the straw quickly toward the heap of soft bodies. Anna's full round buttocks were nearest to me. I raised the riding crop and struck with all my force. She wakened with a gasp, rolling aside and revealing her beautiful front with its soft crotch of jet-black hair. The anger in her eyes died when she saw me. She became seductive, provocative. She was going to have to compete with the others for my lust. At once I thrashed the other two into a waking state. They gasped and screamed slightly, cowering on the straw, but when they saw Anna already awake and attempting to excite me with her lovely body, they changed their attitude. Mona moved forward on her knees and took me in her mouth. When Anna moved forward to stop her, I struck my old mistress once across her soft wheaty belly with the crop which I still held firmly in my right hand. A burst of laughter rang out behind me and the grill closed softly.

Suddenly I pushed Mona away and took Milly's plump little sex in my mouth. She shuddered with ecstasy and bounced like a little balloon on the straw. A moment later, I felt Anna's soft crevice slide against me. I caressed her softly and urged her to puncture herself to the hilt. Mona slipped her thighs silently around Anna's head and the four of us heaved, groaned, and twisted ourselves into ecstasy on the straw.

When it was over, I laughed and joked with them until Kirstin came to take me away. Once outside in the corridor, she made me lie down naked on the stone, my face toward the ground. She gave me three strong strokes on the buttocks. Her hollow, thocking footsteps died away along the corridor.

136

The new maid, Ursula, arrived while I was out with Vivian.

Vivian had nowhere to go that evening so we talked together until nearly seven o'clock.

She spoke with enthusiasm about a European trip which she intended to make in the autumn. I laughed and told her I knew Europe well, Paris, London, Rome, Madrid, Copenhagen, Amsterdam and many other great cities.

She asked me all sorts of questions and laughed delightedly at the answers. Neither of us noticed the passage of time.

"Is Paris really so lovely?"

"Lovelier," I said. "In springtime there is no other place to be!"

"And in autumn?"

"Lovely too," I said. "Arrive at Gare St. Lazare, and go right out into the streets. It's a new smell, a new atmosphere . . . and the cafés are all busy, and they're crammed out front with baskets of oysters and clams and shrimps and people sit outside drinking white wine, especially at evening . . . it's best then, and the sky's a sort of helio color. And then walk up from St. Lazare to Montmarte, go up to the Place du Terte and along to the terrace of the Sacré Coeur and look down across the city. You can see everything, the Seine, the Isle de la Cité, the Isle St. Louis, Notre Dame, the Pantheon, the Louvre, Concord, the Eiffel Tower, the Arc de Triomphe . . ."

I was watching her closely. Her eyes had lit up with pleasure. Good. She was a Romantic. It would probably be very easy.

As I watched her beautiful grey-green eyes, the lovely curve of her cheek under the soft, ash-blonde hair, my heart suddenly went out to her. I really loved this beautiful creature, and a twinge of guilt stole over me. I repressed it at once. It occurred to me that it was precisely the absence of such twinges that made Kirstin my superior. It was right that she should control me. I closed my eyes and imagined my radiant face falling against her belly to suck . . .

"Where are you off to?" Vivian said with a laugh.

"Paris," I said with a smile, "the queen of the world . . . I was just thinking," and my face grew serious and sad, "that I'd have loved to go with you . . . I . . ."

"Why don't you, Saul!" Vivian cried, taking my hand in hers across the table.

I shook my head with a wry smile.

"You know it's impossible, Vivian. It takes me all I've got to keep the house going and your uncle certainly wouldn't release any money for me to go on a trip with you!"

"Oh, please, Saul!" she cried, squeezing my hand. "I have plenty of money, more than I could ever spend! Please come with me! You can be my guide and show me places. It would be much nicer than having nasty old professional ones!"

"I don't think I can, Vivian," I said quietly. "Let's drop it for the moment. We can think about it some other time. Autumn's a long way off. We'll see . . ."

"Promise me to think about it at least!" Vivian said, making a face.

"I promise . . ."

"Oh, it would be *wonderful*, Saul!"

I smiled and nodded, without replying.

"We could do so many things together!"

"Time we rode back, Vivian," I said quietly, looking at my watch. "Lewis dines at eight."

"Oh hell!" Vivian said charmingly. "What a bore! Oh, he's so sweet and good-natured too, Saul, really he is, but he talks all the time about history, and the meaning of words, and about how the American liberal tradition is one of the noblest things in the history of ideas . . . oh, I suppose it's true! And he's so sweet about it! and so concerned about seeing I get everything I want! but I don't really care about all that, Saul! I just want to live and be myself . . ."

"You don't really care?"

"Oh no, of course not!" she said laughing. "Do you?"

I shook my head, allowing her to see that she was making a great impression upon me. At once she reached forward with her other hand and took my hand in both of hers.

"Let me read your palm!" she said. "Yes! It's just as I thought," she said in a mock-serious voice, "You're going on a long journey, probably in the autumn!"

I laughed and squeezed her hand.

"Come on now," I said. "You're going to be late for dinner."

We walked out holding hands to the horses, mounted and rode side by side to where we had parted the previous night. I dismounted. She at once did the same.

"'Bye, Saul," she said, holding out her hand to shake mine. I took it and drew her quickly toward me; I kissed her softly on the lips.

"I'd be a dangerous guide . . ."

In reply she rubbed her soft hair against my mouth . . .

"This is Ursula, Mr. Folsrom."

"Ah, yes! Show her in, Kirstin! I was wondering if she had arrived."

"What age are you, Ursula?"

"Nineteen, sir."

I looked her up and down. She was a tall girl, almost as tall as Kirstin, with fair hair and a solid figure, the muscles heavy and powerful, and she looked puritanical.

"Ursula's a member of the Plymouth Brethren," Kirstin said with a smile. "I told her we wanted a good, careful girl with strict morals and one who is not easily influenced by the wrong kind of people."

"Yes, of course," I said. "I do hope you won't be a disappointment to us Ursula?"

"Oh, no sir!"

"Very good, Kirstin, you had better show Ursula to her room. Kirstin will tell you all about your duties, Ursula."

"Yes sir! Thank you sir!"

They went out.

I waited impatiently for Kirstin to return. She came in about five minutes later. She was smiling.

"What do you think of our new recruit?"

"She looks wholesome. She's probably a virgin."

"Oh, without doubt," Kirstin said with a laugh.

"She may be difficult to corrupt."

"But how much more interesting!" Kirstin said. "When we finally pervert her, think of the fervor she'll bring to her lust! You know, she reminds me a bit of myself when I was young. I think that's why I fell in love with her. Most of the others, perhaps all three, like to have indignities inflicted on them. She's probably cruel. You wait and see!"

I laughed.

"You're wonderful, Kirstin!" I said. "I don't know how I ever lived without you!"

"You didn't," Kirstin said, raising her skirt at the front and showing me her shockingly pale thighs. "Before, you only dreamed . . ."

Chapter 9

$\mathcal{N}$ext time I met Vivian we confessed our love for one another. She did not wish to ride to the hotel as usual.

"Let's go into the woods on your estate instead," she said brightly. "It's such a wonderful day. I don't want to sit in the beastly old hotel lounge!"

I agreed willingly and we rode back to my place and tethered our horses to a fence.

"What wonderful trees!" she exclaimed.

"The elms, yes! My uncle used to be very proud of them."

"No wonder! They must be as old as the hills!"

I laughed, reminded of something.

"Let's go into the woods," I said. "They're pretty extensive."

"Oh, they're beautiful, Saul! How lucky you are to have them!"

I took her hand and we walked deeper into the woods.

"Oh, hold on a minute," I said, "there's something I want to show you!"

"What is it?"

"Wait, we must go out of the woods this way. It's a small copse I used to play in when I was a boy. It's a wonderful place. Completely isolated from the world!"

"How lovely! Is it far?"

"Not far. This way." I took her gently by the hand and led her out of the woods toward the copse. We wended our way through the bushes and came to a halt in the small mossy clearing.

"How wonderful!" Vivian said happily. "It's true. It's as though the rest of the world didn't exist!"

As she turned to face me, I took her in my arms and kissed her passionately on the lips for the first time. She responded warmly at first and then her slim body relaxed utterly in my arms. I kissed her neck and ran my hands through her superb blonde hair. A moment later she slipped down to the ground, drawing me beside her.

She had closed her eyes. Her lovely face was calm, the temples waxen, the soft red lips wet and smooth. Gradually, under my caress, her whole body arched to be taken, but I desisted, simply pulling her blouse out of her riding breeches at the back and caressing her sides and shoulders.

When she opened her grey-green eyes I told her I loved her and that I didn't care what Lewis thought. She smiled submissively and drew my head down to kiss her lips.

That day I didn't make love to her. I felt she was not quite ready to give everything, but we had already spoken of marriage, each of us seeming to hesitate, and we agreed that we should meet again in two days' time, each with his decision.

I rode back with her nearly as far as Lewis' place before I returned to the estate.

Kirstin was waiting for me.

"Seen her again?"

I nodded.

"How is it going?"

"Well."

"I want to know more," Kirstin said.

"It may be necessary for me to go on a European tour with her. Even if we were married soon, she would want to go there for the honeymoon."

Kirstin laughed.

"Why not?" she said. "Two young people in love could have a wonderful time in Europe. And then, when it's all over, you'll bring her back for Kirstin! She'll cause a sensation in the cellar."

I wasn't quite sure that I enjoyed speaking of Vivian like this. I really loved her. But of course, Kirstin was right. Kirstin was always right.

"How's the new maid shaping?"

"Mona made improper suggestions to her last night," Kirstin said with a laugh. "She says she thinks that Ursula nearly gave way. Mona pretended to have a toothache and asked Ursula if she could go into her bed for a while. Ursula agreed, and Mona cuddled up against her with her cheek on Ursula's shoulder. Mona's a clever child!"

I agreed and poured myself a drink.

"Well, a little while later," Kirstin went on, "Mona moved her head down onto Ursula's breasts. She said her tooth was still aching and that she wanted to keep it warm. Ursula didn't resist. It was only when Mona had her cheek on Ursula's naked belly—about two inches from her sex, Mona says—that Ursula finally froze and leapt out of bed."

Kirstin paused to light my cigarette for me.

"Thanks," I said, rather surprised at her thoughtfulness.

"Mona went after her," Kirstin said, blowing out the match. "She actually got her mouth on Ursula's sex, but Ursula kicked her away finally."

I made a face.

"And this morning she came and told me about it."

"Who? Mona?"

"No. Ursula!" Kirstin said. "She said that Mona had tried to seduce her and that she couldn't stay on if Mona stayed."

"How did you get out of that?"

"I asked her to give Mona another chance and when she seemed as though she was going to refuse I asked her if it wouldn't make any difference if I allowed her to punish Mona. 'How?' she said. I told her that I thought Mona ought to have a good whipping and that as she was the injured party, Ursula ought to administer the punishment. Oh, I didn't make any mistakes about that girl! She hemmed and hawed but I could see she was dying to give Mona a whipping!"

I waited eagerly for her to go on. I was speechless with admiration. Machiavelli would have doffed his cap to my Kirstin!

"So I called Mona and scolded her for what she had done and then I told her to fetch a riding crop, that Ursula was going to be allowed to punish her. Mona pretended to be scared, but she loved the idea really. She couldn't wait to get her clothes off. But I thought I might as well arrange things properly. So I took them both down to the cellars. You know that little cellar at the other end of the corridor from the *Lair?*"—I smiled at the name she had given to the women's cell—"Well, I led them in there. I had already got Cliff to fix chains to the wall in there. I thought we might need a place like that sometime. I told Mona to strip, chained her naked to the wall and gave Ursula the riding crop. You should have seen that girl give it to her! Mona screamed blue murder. But she enjoyed it well enough. I congratulated Ursula on her determination. She was feeling very moral but she was obviously in a hot state of sex by that time. So I gave her the key and told her that it was completely up to her how long Mona remained there, chained to the wall like that. I told Ursula that she was to be Mona's warder and feed her during her confinement. Ursula was frantic with joy. I left and left her to it. She was going up and downstairs all day. She couldn't keep away from Mona, can't yet. I think she'll probably sleep down there! The last time I went down I peeped through the grill. They were both naked and Ursula was kneeling in front of Mona, sucking her off."

I burst out laughing.

"You're a genius, Kirstin!"

Kirstin nodded her head calmly.

"At this rate, we should get Ursula into the *Lair* by the end of this week. If we do, I'll get in touch with the other girl and tell her to come a week earlier. I think Anna might have a shot at seducing the new girl. What do you think? Is she ready for that kind of work yet?"

"I'll talk to her and tell you what I think."

"Good. By the way, just as soon as we get Mona and Ursula out of the little cellar, we must go ahead with the branding. I won't feel really secure until these women have been branded."

"What exactly's the idea?"

"Don't be stupid," Kirstin said, getting up and going to the door. "We've got to make these women feel that they *belong.*"

As she closed the door behind her the uncomfortable thought struck me that one day Kirstin might insist on branding me . . .

A chill came to my stomach and I sat there thinking: Would I be able to resist?

Vivian looked pale when I met her two days later.

"What's wrong, darling? Has anything happened?"

"Let's go somewhere where we can talk, Saul."

"Where would you like to go? The copse?"

"No. I think I'd prefer the hotel. It's more impersonal. Let's go at once."

I cantered after her.

When we were seated alone in the small cocktail bar—as yet we were the only customers—she began to speak immediately.

"I told Uncle Elmer that I loved you, Saul, and that we were thinking of getting married."

"Oh God!" I said. "What made you do that?"

"Well, I knew he felt cold toward you but I thought

he had a right to know. Since my father died, Uncle Elmer has been a kind of second father to me. I didn't feel right, somehow, not telling him."

I nodded.

"And what did he say?"

"He begged me not to."

"I'm not surprised," I said dryly. "What did you say to that?"

"I asked him what his reasons were."

"Did he tell you?"

"He didn't want to, but finally he did. He thought it was the only way he could stop me marrying you."

"And will it?"

"I don't know, Saul!" She was nearly in tears. "I don't know what to believe! I love you! But . . ."

"What exactly did he say to you, Vivian? Tell me. I have a right to know."

"Of course you have, Saul!"

"Go on then, darling." I took her hand and she didn't try to escape.

"He said that when you were a boy that woman Anna had a terrible influence over you. He said that you poisoned your uncle because of her, that she might even have persuaded you to do it! Oh, Saul, did you? Did you kill your uncle?"

"Yes, Vivian darling, I killed him. I can't lie to you!"

She squeezed my hand.

"But why, Saul!"

"I loved Anna," I said, "and he pretended that he despised her because she was a Jew."

"Didn't he?"

"He went to her bedroom one night and forced her to strip naked for him. He threatened to have her extradited if she didn't obey him. She came from Russia. God knows what would have happened if she'd been sent back there. Her mother was in a brothel at that time and she probably died there . . ."

I weighed my words carefully, enunciating clearly, and watched the gradual signs of understanding and forgiveness well up in Vivian's beautiful eyes.

"Anna was helpless," I continued. "Uncle Harris had gone into town that day. He brought back with him a pair of black silk stockings, a pair of black high-heeled shoes with ankle straps, and a frilly black garter belt. He made her put them on . . ."

An expression of horror had come to Vivian's eyes. The stray thought passed through my mind that sometime, quite probably in the near future, Vivian would gladly, abasing herself utterly, go through the same humiliating movements. I squeezed her hand.

"Do you want me to go on?"

She nodded urgently.

"He told her to fetch her lipstick. She did. He made her paint the nipples of her breasts with it. Then he made her stand on a chair and he opened her sex and painted her labia."

I allowed time for that to sink in and then I continued: "By the way, I forgot the mask. He made her wear a mask. I can't describe what he did next, Vivian. It was too disgusting. But then he thrashed her with a riding crop, not only on the bottom but also on her sex."

Vivian emitted a gasp of horror.

"And then he violated her," I said shortly, "and his parting words to her were that she should be prepared in the future to perform for him whenever he desired it.

"So I killed him. I loved Anna. It was the only way . . ."

"Oh, how horrible! How humiliating for her! Oh, I don't blame you, Saul! What a terrible thing to happen! And you were only a child! Did you see all this?"

"I saw it through a keyhole."

"Does my uncle know about this?"

"Some of it at least. I think he must. He talked to Anna."

"Then what has he got against you?"

"If only I knew, Vivian!" I said with a tired smile.

She squeezed my hand and went on.

"He said something about this accident."

"Yes?"

"He said that he wasn't sure it was an accident, that you made love to Anna before you killed Inez and that now you've taken Anna again."

I laughed sadly.

"It sounds all so purposive when you put it that way!" I exclaimed. "Well, I did make love to Anna. We hadn't seen each other for years. We fell into each other's arms, and before we knew what we were doing we were making love. Do you understand?"

She nodded, her eyes shining. "With all that passed between you, of course!"

"When it was over, we agreed that she had better go away with her husband as they had arranged to do. She didn't really love me, and I didn't really love her. We said good-bye. It was over. But then the accident happened."

"Tell me about that, darling," she said softly, squeezing my hand again.

"I didn't know Inez from Adam!" I exclaimed. "I saw the man once, at a distance when I was a kid. And anyway, the woods were very dark. I couldn't sleep, you see, so I took my gun and went to the woods. It was just before dawn. I hoped to bag a rabbit or two. Suddenly I heard someone coming through the undergrowth. I got the scare of my life. No one had any right to be in the woods. I waited. And then a man appeared. I couldn't see him properly, just his outline. I told him to stop where he was. I was just going to ask him who he was and what he was doing there when he brought up his own gun and took a pot at me." I tapped my shoulder. "Well, I didn't think as I saw that gun come up. I fired, twice, and at the same time I felt myself struck in the shoulder. Even when I turned him over I didn't know who he was. His face was half blown away. It was a horrible mess. I went back to the house and phoned the police. That's all there was to it. It was like a nightmare."

"Poor darling!" said Vivian, moving closer to me. I put my arm around her and we sat, saying nothing, for a few moments.

"And Anna?" she said at last.

"She's still at my place, and she can stay there just as long as she likes and your damn uncle can go and hang himself!"

She laughed for the first time in a long time. "Poor Uncle Elmer! It's all so easy to understand! He'll come round, Saul. You'll see!"

"Does that mean you're going to marry me?"

"Of course I am, darling! I couldn't live without you! Especially now that I know all about you!"

I laughed.

"There's not much to tell. I'm really a very ordinary person, Vivian."

"And Uncle Elmer even called you mad!"

"Mad?"

"Yes! He said there was a possibility that you were a homicidal maniac!"

"Do I look mad?" I said, looking into her eyes.

"Just mad enough for me!" she said, screwing up her pretty nose, and planting a sweet, soft kiss on my lips.

"You'd better be careful, darling," I whispered, rubbing noses with her, "I may be dangerous . . ."

"You said that before!" she whispered softly. "I think I might like you to be dangerous . . ."

"How did it go?"

"We're engaged to be married. We drove into town and she chose an engagement ring this afternoon."

"You're a quick worker, Saul. Perhaps I'll give you something nice tonight!"

"Oh, old Lewis helped!" I said with a short laugh. "I don't care what he says about me so long as he makes it interesting! A couple more murders wouldn't do me any harm! She'd come and ask me about them and I'd explain and she'd understand, and she *would*! She really would. She's wonderful. I love her very much!"

Kirstin bellowed with laughter. She opened her legs

and nodded for me to come to it. I moved at once and kissed its wet, hairy surface lightly.

"The trouble with young women these days," Kirstin said, "is they've got no moral sense . . ."

✸

"Come down to the cellars. We've got business to do."

I was lying on the couch, my mouth buried at Kirstin's magnificent crotch, and she was seated, her thighs raised, to allow me better access. I didn't want to move at that moment and I pretended not to hear her. She said nothing for a few moments, suffering me to go on with my tongue. And then she said: "Did you hear me, Saul?"

"Yes."

"*Now,* then."

I got up reluctantly, straightened my tie, and followed her down to the cellars.

"This way," she said.

She led me along to the small cellar at the end of the passage.

"The fish is in the net," she said. "This cellar's empty again."

I followed her in.

She pushed the bolt behind us.

"Strip," she said shortly.

I hesitated only for a split second before I obeyed. I stood naked before her.

"Over against that wall," she said. "Stand with your face to it. Between the chains."

A moment later she had clicked the metal cuffs on my wrists and ankles.

"You realize, Saul, that I do everything I do for your own good?"

"Yes," I said huskily, staring at the wall in front of me. I already felt my sex twitching with anticipation.

"You love me and you want to go on loving me and you'd be miserable if you didn't," Kirstin said. "That's why sometimes I have to be cruel. But I do it for my own pleasure too, Saul. I like being cruel to you. I want to humiliate you. And you want to be humiliated, is that not right?"

"Yes," I whispered.

"I'm not doing this because you disobeyed me just now. I'm doing it because I want to hurt you. I'm not going to stop until you scream for mercy, you understand? Look around!"

I looked over my shoulder and saw that she held a thick, black dog whip in her hand. I had an impulse to flee, but the chains prevented me. A moment later I thought my back had split open as the first stroke of the lash crashed out like a pistol shot. I shuddered. What was happening to me? Did I want this? This was mad! insane! My thoughts were interrupted by the sudden knifelike cut at my buttocks. The pain rose up through my entire body and made my head ring. I gritted my teeth. I wanted to say: "Stop it, Kirstin. For God's sake, stop this madness!" but the words didn't come to my lips. The third and fourth strokes followed in quick succession. An agonizing pain swept up the length of my back. I felt that the flesh was hanging from the bones, and horribly, as my head fell, my chin touching my chest, I noticed that I had become hard and that the knob of my member was grazing itself against the stone wall!

After that I was conscious only of pain. I no longer associated it with sex, or with Kirstin. I had no time to think. My mind was filled utterly with excruciating pain. I felt my mouth hang open and I screamed, no longer counting the strokes, borne like a splinter on the tide of my own noise, one livid candle of pain. When Kirstin unlocked me I clung to her as I would have clung to my savior. She eased me down onto the straw, gently, reassuring and gave her hot sex to my lips once again. I was like a baby at its mother's breast and I was glad, glad that I had been hurt now that I was there amongst her softness which she gave to me because she loved me and I belonged . . .

It was half an hour later when she pushed back the grill of the *Lair* and asked me to look for myself. Big Ursula was lying with her belly on the straw near the other women. She was dozing. The other three had been talking quietly to one another. They stopped when they heard the movement of the grill.

"Do you want to take her now or afterward, Saul?" Kirstin said at my shoulder.

"Afterward," I said. "But we haven't decided yet which one's to be branded first."

Kirstin laughed.

"Milly, of course! Always the weakest first! That is a first principle in this kind of thing!"

I nodded.

"Well, let's get it over with," Kirstin said. "I'm impatient to see how she takes it. Inside a week she'll be showing it to the others with pride. You wait and see! . . . Think of when we do it to your pretty new bride!"

I closed my eyes, but no resistance would rise in me.

"Go and heat the iron in the boiler room," she said. "It's standing beside the boiler. 'S' for Saul. I'll get the girl along to the other cellar."

I obeyed. I watched the iron "S" grow white hot in the furnace and I held it at arm's length, staring at it.

I walked along the passage like an automaton to the little cellar at the end. Kirstin was already there and the naked girl was already in her chains.

"Get your dirty little bum out, girl!" Kirstin said as soon as I had closed the door, and putting her shoulder at the young girl's thighs she raised the buttocks into a more accessible position.

"Now, Saul, on the left buttock! Before the iron gets cold!"

I lurched forward, hesitated, and thrust the brand against the soft flesh. The scream that followed seemed to shake even the stone walls of the cellar. Kirstin, still forcing the buttocks up against the brand, had a terrible light of triumph in her eyes.

I pulled the brand away. It had a tendency to cling. It came away with a puff of smoke which smelled of burning meat.

When Kirstin stood up, the girl flopped on the straw. She had fainted. Kirstin threw a blanket over her.

"Leave her here for the night," she said. "We won't

put her back with the others until most of the pain's gone. Then she'll say it wasn't so bad. She'll be proud, you'll see. A mark of distinction. The others'll be jealous. They'll dream about having the same thing."

"Can I not stay with her for a while?"

"Certainly not! You've got work to do! Go now and mount that big Ursula! Give it to her hard! She's a virgin . . ."

Chapter 10

*O*n the six weeks that followed, the branding was completed. Each of five women, Anna, Mona, Milly, Ursula, and the new girl, Jean, had an "S"-shaped scar on her soft left buttock, and all five slept like kittens at night on the straw floor of their *Lair.*

Even I was surprised at the general lack of protest. They accepted without question, even joyfully, every humiliating limitation we imposed upon them.

"The depth of love," said Kirstin with a strange light in her small eyes, "is the fervor of the assent . . ."

"They have security, they know they belong. What more could they wish for?" Kirstin said another time. "Don't be a sentimentalist, Saul; otherwise I'll know that you feel insecure . . ."

I shuddered. I threw myself at once to her soft yielding crotch.

"Face the facts," she said gently. "These women are weak. They want to be loved. Cut out all that rubbish about democracy. There is no democracy in love. One takes; the other longs to be taken. Don't think about what a sexual union 'should' be. See it for what it is. These women have annihilated themselves in relation to us.

They have no more problems. They don't exist. Each day they become more like the animals they always longed to be. They have a nice clean cage with nice clean straw, and they're fed regularly, and looked after . . . no wonder they love you, Saul! Did you ever know an animal that didn't love his master?"

Cliff knocked at the door and entered the library. He carried his skipped cap with "Keeper" written on it in his right hand. Cliff had become very useful. It was he who filled their food and water troughs, washed the women down, and kept them well-groomed. Needless to say, it was his privilege to avail himself of any or all of them when he felt like it. I suspect that he did so quite often for he seldom went into town now, even on his day off. He was also allowed to administer minor punishments for small offenses.

"The stockings and garter belts have arrived, sir," he said. "I was wondering whether you wanted me to fit them immediately?"

"Yes, Cliff. See that they fit well, especially the tops of the stockings around the thighs."

"Yes, sir."

"I'll be down in half an hour, Cliff, to see how they look."

"They'll be ready, Mr. Folsrom."

He went out.

I returned between Kirstin's legs.

"What about your fiancée?" she asked.

"I had a letter from her today. We're to be married in Boston on September second and we sail the same day on the *America* for France."

"What about Lewis? Did she say she had seen him?"

"He's in Boston just now with her. She says he seems to have given up trying to influence her. It's funny. I didn't think he would take it lying down like this."

"What else can he do?"

"I don't know. He knows it would be useless to make the truth of my uncle's death public. He threatened Vivian with that. She said that if he did, she would marry me at once. There'd be no hope of his accomplishing anything then. I'd have every top-flight lawyer in America working for me. That's the advantage of being rich. You can get away with murder. Literally. No, he would only hurry things up if he went to the police about my uncle's death. And anyway, he's reluctant to do so because of Anna."

"What exactly is Vivian worth, Saul?"

"It's difficult to say. She said once that she must have more than seven million dollars."

"And to think it will soon belong to us," Kirstin almost purred. Her hand forced my mouth more tightly against her crotch. "You're a little pig, Saul," she said softly. "You can never get enough of it. Perhaps I'll build a sty for you!"

Later, we went down to the cellars.

Cliff was still down there, surveying his handiwork.

The women looked very pretty and well-groomed indeed. Each wore high heels with ankle-straps, black nylon stockings, and special sealskin garter belts. The nipples of each woman were painted a different color, Anna's red, Mona's green, Milly's blue, Ursula's black, and Jean's a grey-silver. They lounged casually on the straw.

Their *Lair,* inhabited by them for a long time now, had taken on a distinctive odor. It smelled of female, hot, sultry, and slightly oppressive. One had only to smell it to become excited.

"Stand up, you sluts!" Cliff bellowed as we came in.

Ursula, who was not quick enough, received a stroke of the riding crop across her big pearly buttocks.

"Single file!"

The women stood in a line, Ursula, the tallest, in front, and Milly, the smallest, in the rear.

"Now! One, two . . . hop! One, two . . . hop! One, two . . . hop!"

The girls circled us like circus ponies half a dozen times . . . one, two . . . hop, one . . . until Cliff ordered them to stop.

"They're in fine shape, Mr. Folsrom, except that lustful bitch, Anna. She's got the curse."

"Put her in solitary, Cliff. Give her six cuts each day until it's over."

"Come here, you rancid piece of mutton!" he shouted at her. He attached a leash to the collar at her neck and was going to lead her out.

"Just a moment, Cliff. Bring her over here."

I opened my fly and took out my rampant member.

Cliff, gathering my intention, threw Anna on her knees in front of me. She didn't need to be told what to do. Cupping her hands under my testicles as though to catch rain, she took it in her mouth and sucked long and deep with little shuddering grunts of satisfaction.

"Look at her! The dirty little bitch!" Cliff said.

Anna, in an ecstasy of humiliation, moaned softly. Her beautiful red-tipped breasts rose and fell with heavy breathing.

A moment later, my ecstasy leapt boiling into her mouth.

At once Cliff tugged at her leash.

"That's all then! Come on!"

He led her stumbling from the cellar by the leash.

I was just about to go to the dining room for dinner—the new maid, Gloria, had just come to the library to inform me that it was ready—when the front doorbell rang.

Cliff answered it.

He came to tell me that Mr. Lewis had arrived and wished to speak to me. He was in the sitting room.

I joined him there at once.

"Mr. Lewis! It's been a long time!"

We shook hands.

"I've just arrived back from Boston," he said. "I came right here."

"I'm glad you did! I'll tell Gloria to lay another place for dinner."

"All this chopping and changing of servants!" His tone expressed slight disapproval.

"Yes," I said ironically, "it's difficult these days."

"Is Kirstin still with you?"

"Oh yes! I wouldn't let her go for all the gold in China!"

His face relaxed.

"Thank you, Saul. I accept your invitation to dinner. I must talk with you."

"Let's leave it off at least until after the soup!" I said with a laugh.

It was like old times seeing him sitting there at the other end of the long table.

When the fish arrived he began to speak.

"Saul, I want to ask you for the last time to reconsider your decision about marrying Vivian. I am certain she won't be happy with you . . ."

"What the hell do you know about it!"

He was rather taken aback by my violent rejoinder.

"Really, Saul, that's no way to talk to me!"

"You've got a damn nerve!" I said. "You've interfered with me ever since I returned from England. You've insinuated I'm a murderer and you've threatened . . ."

"But you are a murderer, Saul. You murdered your uncle."

"You said as soon as I arrived that you were willing to forget all that. It's lunacy to hold me responsible for it now!"

"Yes," he said rather sadly, "but I have found it isn't so easy to forget. Especially now that you intend to marry my niece."

"She's not even your niece!"

"She's close enough to be my daughter."

"Why don't you be honest?" I said suddenly.

"What do you mean?"

"I mean stop pretending you're against me because I killed my uncle."

"I don't understand . . ."

I smiled disbelievingly.

"You knew my uncle very well, Mr. Lewis. The child in me was on the side of the angels when he destroyed Uncle Harris. You know that very well. No, Mr. Lewis. What you're afraid of is the man the child has become. He bears a striking resemblance to his victim. I'm a true Folsrom. I might almost *be* Uncle Harris!"

He had gone pale.

"So you know then," he said simply.

"Of course I know! Do you take me for a fool? You thought your man, Inez, was trustworthy. You thought he would make a good safe husband for Anna. You were almost in love with her yourself, Mr. Lewis, weren't you? If only you hadn't been a cripple! . . ."

He winced.

I went on. "Oh, it all became quite clear to me when I thought about it later. I remember your very words: 'Look at Anna, my God! Is she decadent or uncreative?' You loved her then, Lewis, and you suspected my uncle's intentions. You probably offered Inez money to marry her. But you weren't quick enough. My uncle was too quick for you. He was there with his whip and his lust and Anna was sprawling naked under him on the bed before you could do anything about it! No. It took a Folsrom to deal with a Folsrom. I was quick enough at the age of twelve. I knew what to do. And you're thinking that if I was quick and dangerous enough to do that at twelve I must be a very dangerous man indeed now. Is that not it?"

He was paler than ever.

"And then there was Inez," I said with a laugh. "You were frightened of my coming back. Inez didn't give a damn for her, and anyway, he was drunk most of the time. And you got your satisfaction that way. You comforted her. You visited her all the time and she wept with her head on your shoulder. That must have been very nice for you . . . all hot and tearful and helpless, crying in your arms! Did you ever touch her thigh, Lewis?"

"You scoundrel!"

"Cut that out, Lewis! It's not even funny. You think if you'd had a man's legs you'd have been so virtuous?"

When he didn't answer, I went on.

"You weren't jealous of Inez. You knew he didn't give a rap for her. But I was different, wasn't I? You fought tooth and nail to get her out of my way. And all the time you pretended you were doing it for her good and mine. What filthy hypocrisy! You! The great American Liberal! You sweated at night, didn't you, when you thought of the possibility of our making love together? But we did, Lewis, we did! Did it never occur to you that I'd be too quick for you? You're an academician, Lewis. You don't know the meaning of action!"

"You're a murderer!"

"Yes, and then I shot your janitor like a dog in the woods—" I laughed to see the expression on his face. "Of course, I had no idea who he was at the time, no . . . it was a happy accident!"

"You fiend!"

"Your Anna belongs to me, Lewis! And then, there's Vivian . . . I love Vivian, Lewis, and I'm going to marry her, and I'm going to kiss her white belly and caress her soft thighs until they open, and then your Vivian will belong to me, too!"

He was sitting back in his chair now, a broken man, all the fight gone out of him. He stared at me glassily, his face grey and old. His breath came with difficulty.

"Perhaps I put poison in your soup, Lewis!"

He croaked and clutched his throat.

I burst out laughing.

"In another minute you'll die," I said. "You're a fool, Lewis! You're a weak, spineless fool! Come, put yourself beside me. Who is Vivian going to choose?"

I walked around the table and helped him to a glass of water. He breathed more easily after that. But he had reached the end of his tether. He was powerless to hinder me now. And he knew it.

I changed my tone.

"Look here, Mr. Lewis," I said in a friendly tone, drawing up a chair beside him, "you're right about me in one way and quite wrong about me in another. Don't worry about Vivian anymore. I'll be kind to her. She will be happy with me. I know what I'm talking about. A man like you has no idea . . ."

He shook his head hopelessly and without looking at me, and in a voice hoarse, almost a whisper, he said: "I don't know, Saul. I don't know . . . I must lie down . . ."

"Of course!" I said. "How thoughtless of me! You must spend the night here!"

I rang the bell.

Gloria appeared.

"Send Cliff to me at once and tell Kirstin to prepare the green bedroom," I said.

A few minutes later, Cliff and I helped Lewis upstairs and put him to bed.

"I'll tell your chauffeur to come back tomorrow for you," I said.

He nodded weakly.

"Go and tell him, Cliff."

Cliff nodded and went out.

When he had gone, Lewis' head fell sideways on the pillow and he said to me: "Can I see Anna, Saul?"

"Of course!" I said. "At once."

I went down to the small cellar and unlocked the door.

Anna was seated on her haunches on the straw, eating food from her manger. She looked up as I entered.

"Lewis is upstairs in the green bedroom," I said. "He's not well. I want you to spend the night with him, make him happy, do you understand?"

She nodded, her dark eyes adoring and suggestive.

"Not now, Anna," I said, seating myself beside her and stroking her soft belly. I took off her collar and kissed her neck. She rubbed her soft face against mine.

"Go now," I said. "Tidy yourself up and go to him. You must make him your creature . . ."

❦

A week later, Lewis still hadn't left. He worshiped Anna, and she handled him as she had handled the child in me.

One day she came and told me that he had asked her to marry him. He hadn't long to live. His death would make her entirely independent. She wanted to know what I wished her to do . . .

It was a quiet little ceremony at which I acted as best man.

"We might as well have his money as well," Kirstin had said.

I agreed. Especially as it didn't seem likely that he would outlast the year.

Before the newlyweds returned in Lewis' car to his own house I took Anna aside and told her I was granting her leave of absence only until the day of Lewis' death. After that, she would return to me, and forever after belong to me utterly. I kissed her tenderly and helped her into the car beside him.

Lewis shook my hand warmly. The poor old man was half out of his mind . . .

When I returned alone to the estate, a letter from Vivian awaited me. Lewis had written to her, withdrawing all his objections to our marriage and apologizing for his previous attitude. He also told her that he was marrying Anna, and that, Vivian supposed, must have had something to do with it. However, one way or another it didn't matter. She loved me and was going to marry me and could hardly wait those few weeks that now remained between the day she wrote and September second when we would be man and wife.

As I laid down the letter I noticed two cuttings in the envelope. I took them out. One had been clipped from *Mademoiselle* and the other from *Vogue*. Both mentioned the coming marriage of the lovely debutante of two years ago, Vivian Lewis, and predicted that our marriage would be the marriage of the month.

I put down the cuttings thoughtfully. It had occurred

to me for the first time that Vivian was a very well-known young woman. Wherever she was, there would be constant visits from lawyers and other highly dangerous people. Simply to remove her to the cellar on our return from Europe, to cut her off from contact with the outside world as had been done in the case of the other women—those women had been carefully chosen because they had no living relatives who were likely to wonder about them—might be very perilous indeed. I knew only too well what old family lawyers were like. They were inquisitive, and they were suspicious of anyone who had anything to do with their clients, and quite often, they took it upon themselves to protect their client against himself. Suppose Vivian's lawyers became suspicious at her almost complete disappearance? Suppose they sent down a private investigator and that he discovered the *Lair*? The thought made me turn cold. And yet, was it possible to do these things by half-measures? Anna was safe enough. The links between herself and myself were too strong to be broken. Even if she changed her mind and decided to set herself up independently on Lewis' death, she would not give me away and it would be relatively easy to tempt her back into the fold. But Vivian was entirely different. She was a young woman used to having her own way, in love for the moment, to be sure, but essentially a free spirit to whom none of the ordinary doors were closed—travel, romance, luxury; these were hers for the asking—and was it likely that she would sacrifice everything to become one of the naked beasts in the cellar? Each of the other women had been essentially insecure, hiding behind mere prettiness, coquetry, grim morals, and in that insecurity lay the key to their self-abasement. They had delivered themselves over entirely to the will of another, like subjects of a totalitarian state, women deprived of a real God, victims of their own fatal isolation. Conflict had died with responsibility. They were "free."

But Vivian, what of her?

Was she—a young woman in perfect health, an acknowledged beauty, with more money than she would ever know what to do with—was she afraid of the responsibility of being herself? Did she too experience a lust, a deadly craving for the amorphous?

Much as I should have liked to think so, I thought it highly unlikely. Not yet certainly. In ten years' time, perhaps, if she had not by that time accepted the painful reality of being an individual, if deceived, disappointed, and powerless even with her great wealth to attain inner peace, she contemplated with the insane courage of a disillusioned woman of thirty the possibility of "dying" to herself in subjecting herself utterly and irrevocably to another's will—as I knew well from my own experience, there was an obscene attraction in this—perhaps then . . .

But meanwhile?

If I retracted nothing and returned to the estate with her, I should either have to go through with it and trust to my own and to Kirstin's strength to dominate her completely (and apart from the possibility I had a strange reluctance to do this) or simply inform her of the presence of the women in the cellar, saying that they belonged to me, were, as it were, my personal property for which I was responsible, explaining to her what after all would be the truth—that it would be the cruelest act of all to give these creatures back to their own dominion?

Could I make her understand this?

Perhaps.

But what about Kirstin?

I was at last face to face with a problem which had been becoming real to me for some time past. Since handling Lewis in the way I had, I had felt a peculiar inner strength take root in my soul. I was beginning to recognize the dangerous truth that I was no longer entirely dominated by Kirstin. She had given me too much scope, too much responsibility. I had learned a great deal from her but there was no doubt that she had made a grave mistake in not dominating me utterly. "The depth of love is the fervor of the assent . . ." She had said that herself, and yet she had failed to keep alive the fervor in me. She should have looked to my humiliation with more system, with more purposiveness. Why had she not branded me? Why had she not lacerated my body and humiliated my soul? Obviously because she wished to use me as an ally in gaining control of Vivian's fortune. She had felt that for the time being at least she could not risk destroying my individuality utterly. Well, that had been a mistake, and a woman in Kirstin's position could not afford to make that kind of mistake. If she were to have said: "Saul, I am now going to do so and so to you, for your own good, to free you from yourself," —no. It was too late. She should have struck sooner. To subject myself would have required a considerable effort of will. I was skeptical. I had ceased to be her creature. Kirstin had lost control . . .

It was sad, very sad, but the truth was that Kirstin's presence in the house, unless she could accept an inferior position, a position somewhat similar to that of Cliff's for example, would complicate matters unnecessarily when Vivian returned with me. But would she accept such a position, and, more urgently, had I any particular use for her in an inferior position? How could I trust her ambition? Well . . .

The alternative?

I thought about that for a long time. I came to the regretful decision that as she knew too much Kirstin had to die.

As soon as this conclusion had been forced upon me, the very thought of putting my head between her hot white thighs even for another night revolted me. I had changed. And yet, if I did not act as usual, prostrating myself before the foulness of her body, she would be quick to realize that she had lost control. She would be desperate, and the desperate are dangerous.

A slow flush crept to my cheeks. It had occurred to me that she had to die at once!

I walked across to my desk and loaded the small Mauser which I kept there. I had no sooner dropped it into my pocket and crossed the room once again toward my armchair when the door opened.

It was Kirstin.

She surveyed me curiously with her small, dangerous blue eyes.

"What is it, Saul? You look upset."

I laughed nervously.

"Nothing much," I said. "The strain of all this business with Lewis, I suppose."

She came into the room slowly and sat in her usual

chair. When I looked at her again I saw that the heavy thighs were exposed, white, meaty, and slightly flatulent. She had raised her skirt to her navel, showing her hairy crotch.

"Come suck," she said. "I want to talk to you."

I moved over obediently and sat between her enormous thighs. She took me by the hair of the head and thrust my mouth against it.

For the first time it tasted sour. Try as I would, I could feel nothing but uneasiness, uneasiness tinged with revulsion. But I acted as if I were in ecstasy, moaning with pleasure and breathing deeply.

"That's it," she said persuasively. "There's my little pig!"

I redoubled my efforts.

"I'm taking you to the cellar, Saul. We have business . . .

I pretended not to hear her and my tongue slipped in between the hair-trimmed lips.

And then I felt myself dragged away by the hair of the head.

"Down to the cellar, Saul!"

I did as she told me, walking in front of her down the stone stairs. At the bottom I waited for her. She directed me to go to the small cellar at the end.

The first thing I noticed was the brazier and the brand.

"You knew it would happen sooner or later, Saul," she said, locking the door behind us. "See!" She lifted the white-hot "K" brand for me to see, and then, with a smile, she pushed it back in the red-hot brazier. "Strip, Saul," she said. "It's for your own good."

"It should have happened sooner, Kirstin. At least a month ago," I said with a small smile.

At once she was on guard.

"What do you mean? Get your clothes off at once, or there'll be no more food for you, you little pig!"

I laughed then.

She was gazing at me with a mixture of fear and hatred.

I slipped the Mauser from my pocket and pointed it at her.

"I'm afraid this is the end, Kirstin."

"What do you mean!"

"You are going to die."

She paled. "You wouldn't dare!" she spluttered.

"You know I'm a killer, Kirstin. You've known it for a long time. You should have taken care not to lose control of me. You have studied power long enough to know that."

Her face seemed to fall to pieces. She fell to her knees.

"No, Saul! No! I'll do anything! You can do anything to me, I promise, I'll be yours! I'll help you! Anything! Anything, Saul! Please! Please don't kill me!"

"Strip, Kirstin!"

She hurried to obey me and soon she was standing there, big, shuddering in every fold of flesh, white. Her spiders for the first time looked ridiculous.

"Turn around and kneel down, Kirstin."

Shuddering, she obeyed. She thought she was going to be branded.

I took careful aim and shot her twice through the back of the neck. Her heavy torso jerked twitching forward onto the straw. The blood seeped from an ugly hole just below the hairline at the back of her neck.

❧

"Come in, Cliff, I want to talk to you."

Cliff entered the library.

I pointed to the whiskey and soda. "Help yourself to a drink, Cliff."

"Thanks."

He poured himself a drink and sat down opposite me.

"I've got a problem, Cliff, and I want your advice."

"Sure, Mr. Folsrom. Glad to help!"

I nodded.

"As you know, Cliff, I'm to be married in a few weeks' time. Miss Lewis is a very rich woman, richer even than I shall be myself at the age of thirty when the estate finally comes under my control. You would understand if I said I didn't wish to lose Miss Lewis?"

He grinned.

"Good," I said. "Now, I don't know whether you know exactly what the relationship between Kirstin and myself has been?"

He hesitated. He looked slightly afraid.

"Go on, Cliff. You won't lose by being honest with me."

"I don't know why, Mr. Folsrom, but she seems to think she's got you just where she wants you. She once said to me she had you in the palm of her hand."

"She has, Cliff. And for that matter, so have you."

"Me?"

I laughed.

"Don't worry, Cliff. You're my right hand, you know that. You're too smart to play Kirstin's little game. You know when you're onto a good thing"

"I sure do!" he grinned. "I kinda like being a Sultan."

I laughed. "The harem will grow, Cliff, the harem will grow!"

"Can't ever get too big for me!" he said.

I filled his glass.

"That's why I like you, Cliff," I said. "You and I are birds of a feather, eh?"

He sniggered, relaxing. "Sure," he said, "you and me know what we want!" He stopped, a thought striking him. "What's that bitch up to? Blackmail?"

"Right," I said.

He swallowed his drink.

"If you don't pay up, she stops the marriage. Is that it?"

"Just that," I said. "That's the problem. Now, before you say anything, I want to go on. When I return here with my wife, I think I can get her to accept the women in the cellar, you understand?"

He whistled.

"I'll have four months to work on her. But if she found out before I was good and ready to tell her, it'd be all up with the marriage."

"Sure. I get it. I wouldn't've believed any woman wanted to be in that cellar, but I know different now. I take my hat off to you, Mr. Folsrom."

"There's strange things in this world, Cliff."

His face was hard. "What are we going to do about *her*, Mr. Folsrom?"

I walked over to the safe and returned with a bundle of notes. I tossed it into his lap.

"That's two thousand dollars, Cliff." I took the Mauser out of my pocket and laid it on a table by his side. "In five minutes we are going down to the cellar together and each of us is going to shoot her just once. That way we can trust one another, do you understand?"

He nodded his head nervously, fingering the money.

"Sure, I get you, Mr. Folsrom."

"Then we'll dig a big hole and fill it with half a dozen of those bags of quicklime we've got in the garage, and we'll cover her up, and that will be that. There's no danger, Cliff. No one ever comes near the estate since Inez died."

He nodded. He licked his lips.

"Take another drink."

We drank together, clinking our glasses.

"To a corpse," I said.

He laughed nervously.

"There's nothing to worry about, Cliff, you understand? Money talks. When I'm married to Miss Lewis we'll have more money than we know what to do with."

"Yeah . . . yeah . . . sure . . ."

"Let's go then. I locked her in the cellar an hour ago."

I lifted the Mauser and we went down the stairs, the same stairs which Kirstin had descended for the last time a little over an hour before.

When we reached the small door I said: "I'm going to shoot first, Cliff. Then I'll pass the gun to you and you'll shoot. Got it?"

He grunted assent. I could feel his nervousness.

I opened the door slightly, cautiously, and fired at Kirstin's body which I had propped up in a chair. I passed him the gun. He leaned forward nervously, glanced once at the woman he supposed was his victim, and fired. At once he leaped back into the passage. I peered in.

"Good for you, Cliff! You got her right in the back of the neck!"

He was standing with a stupid smile on his face, still holding the gun. I took it from him and put it into my pocket.

"Now go and find a good place . . . the center of the copse would do. Do you know it?"

He nodded.

"Make it deep, Cliff. I'll get the body ready for carting out there. It'll be easier in two bits."

Cliff vomited.

I patted him on the back.

"Don't let it get you down, Cliff. Go on now, and let's get this over with . . ."

e had been tempted to go to our stateroom ever since the liner sailed out from New York. Occasionally, in quiet places, I had caught Vivian in my arms and held her close to me, smelling her subtle perfume which mingled with the warmth of her fresh young body, and rubbing my cheek on her soft blonde hair. Each time I did so, she would wriggle playfully out of my arms and laugh, throwing her hair back and looking at me mischievously with her lovely grey-green eyes. Even then I had not seen her delightful fawnlike body naked, and now the evening had fallen and land was long out of sight and there was nothing but this floating island of music and gay-colored lights which bore us swiftly toward Europe. We had eaten dinner with champagne of a priceless vintage, our private wedding breakfast, and forgotten the elaborate ceremony of the morning in Boston.

"Thank God it's over!" Vivian had breathed afterward as our black Cadillac shot forward away from the crowds, trailing a string of tin cans.

During the drive from Boston to New York I kissed her until she grew hot and wet with passion, but it would have been improper to make love in front of, or rather

181

behind, the chauffeur who had a good view of us in the rear mirror, and so we desisted, contenting ourselves with interminable teasing which took more out of us than would have the act of love itself.

Now we moved across the deck and stood close at the guardrail. My arm went around her protectively and she gazed up into my eyes. A soft wind blew to us from the sea. We kissed.

"Are you glad?" she asked softly.

"Yes. I thought it would never happen."

"So did I. Time passed so slowly! But then I knew it would be all right when Uncle Elmer married Anna."

"Yes."

"How did that happen, Saul? Did you have anything to do with that?"

I laughed and kissed her.

"I'll tell you all about it some other time!"

She stroked my cheek.

"I think you probably *are* dangerous, Saul," she whispered lovingly. "Uncle Elmer is always right about these things, but I don't care. I love you more than I ever loved anybody."

"You don't know what a risk you're taking, my darling . . ."

She stopped my mouth with a kiss.

Awhile later I asked her if she would like a nightcap before we went to bed.

"Oh yes, I would!" she said gaily, and taking me by the hand she led me into the cocktail bar. "See! There are still two stools at the bar. Let's sit there!"

We toasted one another silently.

Vivian finished her drink first.

"I'm going now," she said. "You follow in five minutes."

She wouldn't listen to my protests.

I was left alone.

§

I had four long months to tell her of the women in the cellar, four months during which I would use every subtlety to make her receive the news without shock or protest. I would be aided by the fact that I doted on her, and that if she loved me now she would be hopelessly in love with me by the time our honeymoon was over.

My mind flashed back to Cliff who would have to control the women by himself during my absence. That was the one disadvantage of Kirstin's death. She was a far more subtle tyrant than ever Cliff could be. Before I had left, however, I had taken Ursula to bed with me three nights in succession and the young girl was now completely under my influence. I had told her that I would be away for four months and that I was depending on her to help Cliff keep everything in order until I returned. She swore she would. But she didn't think there would be any trouble. The girls were happy. She had never heard anyone express the wish to escape.

"You know I do this for your happiness, Ursula darling?" I said softly, stroking her thigh and fingering her sex tenderly. "But if it ever got out, I should get into trouble."

She was breathing heavily, her thick body exuding a

hot sweat. Huskily she told me there was no need to worry, that she would see to it personally that everything went smoothly.

I felt better after that. I pushed her thighs open with my knees and sank into her strong, sponge-soft mound up to the hilt.

Cliff told me not to worry. In the three weeks since Kirstin's death he had regained his courage. He knew now that there was almost no possibility of the truth's ever coming out. And he was happier with Kirstin out of the way. He himself was now in complete control except when I was there, and we had on no occasion found anything to quarrel about.

"Good luck!" he said as I took my departure. "I hope it all works out with you, Mr. Folsrom."

"It will, Cliff, it will!"

Nothing had happened to lower my confidence.

Sitting in the bar, twisting my drink in my hands, waiting for five interminable minutes to pass, I only hoped that for his own sake Cliff would never attempt to blackmail me.

A matter of life and death was no problem to me now. One had simply to be careful, to keep one's nerve, and to strike without warning.

Ah! such thoughts on a man's wedding night!

I was married. Vivian was mine. And her fortune. I think it would have been true to say that I should have loved her just as much had she been penniless. But that wasn't so, and for that I thanked my stars.

Another drink?

Yes. I decided to have one more. I ordered it and drank it at a gulp.

I left the bar and made for the stateroom.

Now, I was thinking, now! It was only the beginning.

She would smell fresh as flowers, only warm, womanly.

I knocked at the door.

"Come in!"

She was standing, half shy, half proud in her black nylon negligee. Her blonde hair swept down to her shoulders like a cascade of soft silver. She was wearing high heels.

I crossed the room quickly and held her in my arms.

She pushed me gently away and allowed her negligee to fall off her shoulders like a pool at her feet.

"Am I beautiful?"

My eyes fell from the red-tipped nipples of her soft-lined breasts to the dainty black garter belt slung at her little belly, downward to the sheer black stockings that clung to the smooth creamy flesh of her thighs.

I glanced up quickly.

In her lovely eyes lurked a knowledge.

I swept her into my arms and carried her across to the bed and a moment later lay naked in her arms, the lights out, and her soft mouth against my own.

I stroked her in silence.

"What would you say if I told you that I have a large

cellar at home," I said, "and that the floor is covered with straw on which five naked women sleep, waiting . . . ?"

She laughed softly.

"Only five?" she said, rubbing her warm belly against my own . . .